THE
RIVER
-OF-
CATTLE

❧ THE WILL AND BUCK SERIES: BOOK I ☙

To Keri,
Hope you enjoy!

Alice V. Brock

ISBN: 978-1-68313-027-7

First Edition

Printed and bound in the USA

Cover and interior design by Kelsey Rice

THE
RIVER
-OF-
CATTLE

❧THE WILL AND BUCK SERIES: BOOK I❧

BY
ALICE V. BROCK

Ⓟ
Pen-L Publishing
Fayetteville, Arkansas
Pen-L.com

DEDICATION

This book is fondly dedicated to the cowboys and cowgirls that galloped through my classroom in Iola, Texas. Like Will holds Buck's reins, you will always hold the reins to my heart.

ACKNOWLEDGMENT

Thank you, Sherrill Nilson, my sister. You are my coach, my cheerleader, and my writing partner. You are an integral part of this adventure. Without you, *The River of Cattle* would be only an empty, dry creek bed.

The encouragement from my critique partner and my friend, Marianne Gage, whose comments and suggestions are always spot on, kept me on the right track.

A special thank you to award-winning author Jodi Thomas, Tim Lewis, Margie Lawson, and the West Texas Writers' Academy for teaching me how to write and for helping get me from my fumbling first draft to a finished book.

Thank you to my family for their support and for my beautiful writing cabin that has become my hideaway and is steeped in Western inspiration.

I am grateful to Duke Pennell, editors Brian and Meg, and Pen-L Publishing for giving *The River of Cattle* a chance.

THE REMUDA

"Come on, Pa. If we don't spur up, the wild horses will be broke before I get there." Will Whitaker's heels itched to tap Buck into a gallop. Yesterday had been all about hurry up and get the work done. Will slipped another side glance at Pa. Today there was no hurry up in the man.

"It's going to be a long day. You want to burn Buck out before we get started?" Pa asked. "I'm gonna need you two on the way back. Besides, we aren't buying wild horses. Goodnight and I need working stock for the cattle drive."

They crested a hill, and Will spotted the corrals in the distance. He gave Buck a slight kick with his boot heels, and the stallion stepped out ahead of Pa's sorrel. Pa didn't seem to notice. The last quarter mile stretched forever.

They rode up to Charlie Goodnight at Baxter's ranch. Horses milled in the loaded corrals, except the big pen in the middle. It held only one. Will forced his gaze from the horse in the pen and turned to greet the tall trail boss. Goodnight was still on his horse. *We're not too late.*

"Good to see you, Dan." Charlie shook Pa's hand.

"Howdy, Will." The trail boss's big hand surrounded Will's. "You ready to be a drover on a long cattle drive?"

"Yes, sir."

As far back in his eleven years as he could remember, Pa had told stories about the famous cowman. He hoped his grin disguised his grimace as the big hand closed with a tight grip. He wiggled his numb fingers and maneuvered Buck closer to the action in the pen.

He watched a bowlegged cowboy walk up to the angry, white-eyed mustang. The blowing, snorting horse stood snubbed to the post in the middle of the corral; sweat already streaked his shoulders. The rider gathered the reins in one hand, stuck one foot firmly in the stirrup, and swung his other leg over the saddle. The cowboy at the horse's head pulled the rope loose and scrambled for the rails. The horse jumped and kissed the moon.

"Ride that bronc!" Will whooped and waved his hat in the air. Snapping the well-worn Stetson tight on his head, he nudged Buck closer and stretched tall in the stirrups to see over the men standing on the corral rails. Billowing dust rose from the horse's hooves like steam. The cowboy was jerked up, down, and sideways. The horse crow-hopped, twisted, and bucked from one end of the corral to the other.

"Buck, did you see that?" Excitement made him wiggle in the saddle, and he slapped his leg with his hat.

The buckskin stallion turned his ears back toward his best friend.

Will pulled his boots from the stirrups and onto the saddle beneath him. Straining to see every second of the action and his heart jumping with every leap of the bronc, he practically stood on the saddle.

"Pay attention. You might learn something about buckin'. Hold tight! Hang on!" He hollered along with the men who rooted for the rider from the safety of the tall bars.

"Pa," Will yelled over the noise of the cheering cowboys. "If all the horses are like that one, I may be the only cowboy not getting a buckin' lesson in the mornings."

"I wouldn't be so sure," said Pa. "You won't be on Buck all the time. You'll have to ride other horses."

Will watched the bronc slow to a walk, horse and rider both sweat soaked. Finally it stopped, front legs spread, head drooping, sides heaving. After a few minutes, the rider nudged it into a walk around the corral.

"Here he is, boys, gentle as a newborn foal." He tipped his hat to the men.

Will patted Buck's neck. "You know, Buck, I can handle horses. I taught you, and you're bigger than any horse here. I can handle anything they put me on."

Two cowboys lassoed a wild-eyed pinto and dragged it, kicking and bucking, to the snubbing post, and the circus started over.

Will wiped his sweaty forehead with his sleeve. He worked his tongue around his mouth to stir up enough spit to swallow. *Well, almost anything.*

"Howdy, Baxter," Pa said as the stoop-shouldered horse trader walked over to Buck. He gave Pa a quick glance, a brief handshake, no greeting. He ignored Will and ran his hand over the buckskin's rump.

Buck sidestepped.

Baxter ran his hands over the muscular shoulders.

Buck snorted, threw his head up, and sidled away.

"You have a fine horse here, Dan," Baxter finally spoke. "But he's too much for this boy." Stepping back, he admired the stallion. "He's got to be at least seventeen, maybe seventeen and a half hands. What is he, five or six years old? Sell him to me. I need a good stallion."

Will shifted in the saddle, not taking his eyes off the man.

Pa dismounted, tied his horse to the corral, and stepped between Baxter and Buck.

"He's not mine to sell. He's Will's." Pa laughed. "Even if you could buy him, you'd be beggin' for your money back."

"Why's that?" Baxter asked, giving Will a startled glance.

"They grew up together. No one else can ride him, not even me. Will was five when Buck was born. The mare died. Will kept slipping out of the house at night. I'd find them bedded down together in the straw, sound asleep."

"Mr. Baxter," Will said. "People have tried to buy Buck before. He and I are partners." He took a deep breath. "Pa never worries about me when I'm with Buck. We look out for each other. You don't sell your best friend."

"I've never seen a horse so taken with a boy, or a boy so taken with a horse." Pa's voice left no room for misunderstanding.

Baxter looked up at Will and shrugged. "You got a fine horse, boy."

Goodnight laughed. "Now, how about the horses we need for the drive to New Mexico?"

Will and Buck followed the three men to the stock pens. "Don't you worry, Buck. Nobody will ever take you away from me." He patted the muscular neck.

Goodnight and Pa took their time looking over the horses and pointed out the ones they wanted. The cowboys separated each one chosen and drove it into the next pen.

"Look at that gray mouse-colored one, Mr. Goodnight." Will pointed across the pen. "He's chunky and not too tall, but he looks strong. See how he holds his head up. Nothin' gets by him."

"That color horse is called a grullo. He's a good one. Baxter, throw a saddle on him. I'll see what he can do."

Mr. Baxter spoke to one of his cowboys, who drove the gray into the corral. The stocky horse snorted and showed the whites of his eyes. The man headed his way, shaking out a loop in his rope.

"He's a wild one." Baxter shook his head. "We've been working with him, but he won't calm down."

Will and Buck took their place at the corral gate. Again, he stretched tall in the stirrups, eager to get a better view of the show. "This ought to be good, Buck. You watch that horse. He'll give you another lesson on buckin'."

The loop settled over the gray, and the cowboy snubbed him to a post. He slipped the hackamore over his head. Another cowboy threw on the saddle, cinching it tight around the horse's belly.

Goodnight grabbed the hackamore, pulled the grullo's head around, put his foot into the stirrup, and swung into the saddle. The cowboy jerked the slipknot loose and ran for the corral bars.

Horse and rider spun in circles. Dust flew in a whirlwind. The grullo bucked straight up. Goodnight settled deeper in the saddle. The horse twisted in every direction. Goodnight hung on.

"Ride him, Mr. Goodnight!" Will yelled. He watched flying hooves and arms slash and flash all over the corral.

"Stick to him!" Pa yelled.

Cowboys whooped and waved their hats.

The horse stopped bucking, snorted, threw his head up, and took off at a dead run. A cowboy threw open the corral gate.

Buck and Will barely scrambled out of the way before the grullo pounded past with Goodnight stuck tight to the saddle. Will jerked the reins. Buck spun on his hind legs, and they tore across the prairie close behind. He was determined to see every bit of this ride.

Will spotted a deep ravine ahead. Wide-eyed, he watched

Goodnight grab a handful of mane, ride the grullo over the edge, and disappear.

Will pulled hard on Buck's reins. They slid to a stop at the rim of the ravine, Buck practically sitting on his tail.

"Whoa, Buck. Did you see that? Yee-haw!"

The grullo landed in mud up to his belly, got his footing, and scrambled up the other side of the creek, hooves throwing mud everywhere. Goodnight, muddy and wet, bent low over the horse's neck, as if to speak in his ear. Horse and man disappeared over a hill and were swallowed by the prairie.

Will and Buck headed back to the corral at a gallop. "Pa," he yelled and pulled Buck to a stop next to Pa's sorrel. "You'll never believe what Mr. Goodnight and that grullo did. That crazy horse leaped off that bluff and kept right on going! You said Goodnight was one of the best bronc busters in Texas, and you were right."

After a time, Goodnight and the sweating grullo came walking back to the corral, covered in mud, both breathing hard.

"I believe I'll take this horse, Baxter. He was as determined to throw me as I was to keep my seat. When he landed in the mud, I thought the ride was over. But he pulled himself out, and away we went. He's got spirit. I like that in a horse."

Goodnight rode into the corral and dismounted. He handed the reins of the sweating horse to a cowhand.

"Cool him down and turn him in with my others. Oh, and check him over." Goodnight patted the horse. His voice dropped. "You've got quite a heart."

"Dan," Goodnight said, "these horses and the ones we're holding at the herd will give us a remuda big enough to start the drive. Let's head 'em out. I'll take point. You ride flank. Baxter, I'll need a couple of men for flank on the other side and for drag."

Will tapped Buck with his heels. The big horse stepped in front of the trail boss. "Mr. Goodnight, I can ride drag. Buck is a good horse. He knows his business, and so do I. We'll keep those horses going."

The trail boss studied Will's set face. "Can you handle that horse of yours? Drag is not an easy job."

He patted Buck's neck and sat taller in the saddle. "Yes, sir."

"Okay. The job is yours. Baxter, I only need one man. I've got one drag rider right here."

Baxter's cowboys drove the horses through the gate. Goodnight and Pa headed them across the prairie toward the holding grounds for the cattle drive. Will and Buck fell in behind the horses streaming out of the corral.

"Can you believe Goodnight liked a horse I picked?" Will asked Buck, not sure he could believe it himself. "And he gave us a job. I wish I could tell Ma. This is the best day ever."

A big sorrel broke away and headed back the way they'd come. Buck turned sharply, cut him off, and drove him back into the herd. Will stuck in the saddle like a grass burr. Another horse dragged behind, and he kicked Buck after him.

Dust from the dry prairie rose from under the horse's hooves. Will pulled his bandana over his nose, hoping to keep out of his mouth some of the grit that his broad smile seemed to keep letting in. Nothing could get away from him and Buck today.

The long, hot afternoon had passed before he spotted the cattle herd. When the last straggler joined the remuda, Will loped Buck over to Pa and Goodnight.

"Thanks, Will," the trail boss said. "You and Buck kept them bunched just right. You'll do fine."

Will's chest swelled till he thought it would burst at the words from the famous cowman. "What do you think about that, Buck?" The grit on his face and in his teeth didn't bother him so much anymore.

"Head on over to the chuck wagon." Goodnight pointed toward the cattle herd. "It's camped under some cottonwood trees about a quarter mile east of here. Tell Cookie who you are, and get yourself a cool drink of water. Eatin' dust on drag makes a man thirsty."

Will looked at Pa.

"Go ahead, son," said Pa. "But go easy. These cattle are restless. This is not their range, and they have a hankering to go home. It'll take a while before they're trail broke."

Cattle stretched as far as Will could see. Some milled around, some grazed, some lay on the ground chewing their cud. Drovers circled the herd, keeping an eye out for any critters wanting to return to home ground.

Will started for the chuck wagon, but then he yanked the reins. The big horse shook his head and rattled the bit in his mouth.

"Sorry," Will said and patted his neck.

He looked back at the herd. Dust hung thick in the air. "Buck, this is it. We're going on a cattle drive."

Cattle drive. The words seemed to echo across the prairie.

SOLD

Pa's words ricocheted off the walls, filling the cabin like a swarm of wasps.

"You sold the ranch?" Will's knees buckled. He sat down hard on the rope-bottomed chair. For some reason, his mouth wouldn't close. He rubbed his eyes, trying to clear his thoughts.

"What about me, Pa?" A pain started in the middle of his forehead and moved around his head in a tight band. "When Ma died, you said I was your partner." His breath stuck in his chest. "If I'm a partner, you should have asked me." He clamped his jaws so hard his teeth ached.

"This chance just came up yesterday while we were looking at horses at Baxter's." Pa sat across from Will at the kitchen table, his callused hands restless, his brown eyes penetrating—begging him to understand. "New Mexico is fresh country. We can start over there."

"You *sold* it?" he asked again. He couldn't feel anything. He couldn't think. He couldn't understand.

"Yes. To Baxter."

"Why? Why did you sell it? Why do we have to start over? Why can't we stay here?" Will's stomach felt like it had that time a stolen bite off Pa's plug of tobacco made him throw up.

"I've told you before things are bad in Texas since the war ended. The Yankees have taken everything."

Will's head dropped to the tabletop. The crumbs from his toast stuck in his dark-blond hair. "I'm sick of hearing about Yankees. That's all you talk about anymore."

"Look at me, Will." Pa took a deep breath. His tone was flat, like he'd said it a hundred times before. "Nobody's buying cattle. If we stay here, we'll lose it all."

Pa stopped talking. He rubbed his forehead hard with the heel of his hand.

"Goin' with Charlie will give us a chance. The army's paying good for beef in New Mexico."

Lifting his head to Pa's work-lined face, Will's eyes pooled with unshed tears. "I'm eleven, Pa. I'm not a kid. You always said this was my ranch as much as yours. Is that true? Or was it a lie?" The last word snapped like a brittle stick.

"Baxter just made the offer yesterday." Pa's voice softened. "We don't have a choice, Will. We can't pay the high taxes put on us since we lost the war against those Northern Yankees."

Will turned away. His thin legs swung back and forth, not quite reaching the floor, his heels slamming the chair leg with each swing.

"If I could have told you sooner, I would have. But the chance just came up yesterday."

"When do we have to go?"

"By the end of next week, when the drive starts."

Will traced a crack that wound like a ribbon across the plank tabletop. His blood roared in his ears and pounded behind his eyes.

Then, as though someone had pulled a plug in his heel, the blood drained from his face, making his head swim. He sat straight up. "Ma!" That tobacco feeling hit him again. "What about Ma? Are you just going to leave her here?" His throat was so tight his voice rasped in a hoarse whisper.

Pa didn't answer.

The clock chimed the half hour. Will watched the pendulum swing—right, left, right, left. All sound faded except the ticking of the clock. There was only a table width between them, but it seemed like miles of prairie.

Finally, Pa whispered, "I don't want to leave her, either." He ran his fingers through his thick sandy hair, making it stand up.

Will looked at Pa's slumped shoulders. His stomach hurt. His head swam. His eyes blurred.

"We have no choice." Pa's gaze drifted away from Will and out the open door. "Your mother would want us to go."

Will stood, the back of his knees slamming into the chair. It teetered and banged to the floor. "No. She. Wouldn't!"

He ran from the cabin, across the dusty yard to the empty corral. Where was Buck? The creak of the open corral gate drifted across the ranch yard.

LEAVING HOME

Tall grass grabbed at Will's chaps as he ran across the prairie. His legs pounded the hard cracked ground. *Why?* rang in his head with every step. *No!* with every pump of his arms. He ran up a small hill, bent over, gripped his knees, and sucked in gulps of air. His lungs aching, he dropped to the ground and sat with his head in his hands. "I can't do it. I can't go." The words escaped between gasps of air. "I can't leave."

When he could breathe easily again, he stood, picked up a fist-sized rock, and threw it—hard. *First, Pa got stupid and sold the ranch without talking to me.* He walked farther out on the prairie. He wondered how his legs could work because they were empty. He felt like a cicada hull he had found one time stuck to a tree trunk. It looked like a cicada on the outside but was empty on the inside. Empty, like Buck's corral. Empty, like their cabin since Ma died. Empty, like Pa.

Then, Buck got stupid and ran off just when I need to talk to Ma. What else will go wrong today? A slight breeze cooled his hot face.

"Buck!" he called.

The empty prairie held nothing but sunburned prairie grass. He turned to the stand of oaks along the creek. Putting his fingers to his lips, he whistled—loud and shrill. Ma had taught him to whistle and taught Buck to come at the sound of it. He and Ma—they had been real partners. They had saved Buck when the mare died. They had convinced Pa to keep the weak little colt. They had raised Buck.

His big, powerful stallion burst from the trees and came to Will. The horse lowered his head. Will wrapped his arms around Buck's neck and buried his face in the long mane, breathing in the familiar dusty smell. *What am I going to do? I can't just leave Ma here by herself.*

He stepped back, and Buck flicked his head. Will's hat hit the ground.

"Don't do that." Will picked it up, twisting it in his hands. "I don't feel like playing." He settled it on the back of his head so it wouldn't add to his stupid headache.

Will reached up, put his hand on the soft velvet nose, and pulled the horse's head down to look him in the eye. "Stop opening the stupid corral gate any time you want out. I had to run all the way out here to find you. I'm already mad at Pa. Do you want me mad at you, too?"

Morning sunshine crept toward its promise of greater Texas heat. The friends stood together. The stallion strong. The boy stunned with grief.

Buck nudged Will, bringing him out of his stupor.

"I thought Pa and me were partners. He sold the ranch to Mr. Baxter." Will heard the sad coo-coo-coo of a mourning dove coming from the creek. "What are we gonna do? Where are we gonna live?" He sucked in a lungful of air and held it.

No answers. Only the loud silence of the Texas prairie.

He blew his breath out.

The slight morning breeze faded. Tilting his hat farther

back on his head to shade his neck from the sun's hot needles, he looked across the prairie toward home.

"Come on." Will scratched under Buck's mane. "We have to go tell Ma good-bye." His hand rested on Buck's shoulder as they walked toward the barn.

He could see Pa at the corral, waiting with Buck's gear. Will took the bridle Pa handed him. He settled the bit in Buck's mouth, slipped the headpiece over his ears, and fastened the buckle.

"This is the right thing to do, son."

Unable to speak, Will pulled the saddle blanket from the top rail and tossed it onto Buck's back.

Pa smoothed it in place. "We can start over in New Mexico."

Will didn't want to hear those words. "What I think doesn't matter. The ranch is already sold."

Without another word, Pa threw the heavy saddle on the horse and tightened the cinch. He cupped his hands and boosted Will into the saddle.

The boy rode out of the yard and down the narrow road. Leaning forward, he urged the big horse into a lope. *He can't do this. He can't. He can't.* The words stabbed his head with each strike of the horse's hooves.

Out of sight of the ranch, Will pulled Buck to a slow walk. The sun burned through his shirt. Sweat trickled down his back. He rode into a meadow filled with sunflowers surrounding a cemetery that backed up to a shady grove of live oaks.

"Look, Buck, Ma's favorite flowers."

The reins dropped to the ground when he slid off the horse to pick the bright-yellow blooms. He could see her smile in the cheerful face in the sunflower. He could feel her touch in the soft golden petals. He could remember her scent in the smell of summer that surrounded him.

I wonder what happened to the sunflower seeds we were gonna plant by the front porch.

The prickly hairs on the stems made his hands itch. He scratched them against his pants leg. "No use thinkin' about seeds," he said to Buck. "We won't have a porch."

Will opened the cemetery gate and walked down the dirt path between rows of simple rough-hewn stone and wooden markers. In the shade of an old live oak, he knelt before a grave and sifted the raw dirt piled there through his fingers. He traced the carved words on the sandstone marker.

Joanna Whitaker and Infant Daughter
February 23, 1839—May 10, 1866
Beloved Wife of Dan, Loving Mother of Will

Will brushed the dust off the stone. The last couple of months, he had gotten used to the weight of his grief. He wore it on his shoulders like a yoke. Now anger made it burn and chafe once again. He picked up the wilted flowers from last week and tossed them over the fence. They burst apart when they hit the ground, scattering dry petals through the brown grass. Carefully, he laid the fresh golden sunflowers against the marker.

He leaned against the back of the stone. The familiar comfort he always felt sitting there did not come. *How can we leave her? I don't even know where New Mexico is.*

The shadows moved slowly across the cemetery, and still he sat. He watched a lone buzzard in the cloudless sky. The empty hole in his heart seemed to grow with each of its widening circles. Will took off his hat and wiped the sweat from his forehead. He rubbed his fingers over his mother's name again. Twisting his hat in his hands, he made circles in the dirt with his boot.

"I have bad news." His mouth felt like it was full of prairie dirt. He wished he'd brought his canteen. "Pa sold the ranch to . . . Baxter." He spit the last word. "We're moving to New Mexico, wherever that is. I don't see why we have to move. Why we can't come back home." He couldn't tell which was worse, his banging head or that tobacco stomach.

Who's going to bring you sunflowers now? Finally, he blew a big sigh, then headed back down the dusty path. Buck moved to the gate to meet him.

The crackle of twigs and leaves from behind jerked him around.

An Indian, long feathers dangling from his hair on both sides of his face, hurdled tombstones as he ran for the gate— and Buck. Will raced across the cemetery. He got to the fence ahead of the Indian, leaped to the top rail, and vaulted into the saddle. The Indian grabbed his boot. Will hung onto the saddle horn with both hands and kicked hard.

Buck whirled and bolted into a full gallop. His hooves shot rocks and gravel behind them. Will grabbed the flying reins, and they fled down the narrow road toward home. He looked back over his shoulder. The Indian stood at the gate, watching them ride away. Feathers, braided in his long brown hair on both sides of his face, blew in the wind.

Will raced into the ranch yard and pulled a sweating Buck to a stop, throwing up a billowing cloud of dust. He kicked his feet free of the stirrups and leaped to the ground.

"Indians!" he yelled and raced toward Pa, dragging Buck behind him. "Indians at the cemetery!"

Buck threw his head, snorted, and pawed the ground.

"He tried to steal Buck!" He patted the excited horse on the neck. "He ran out of the woods straight for him." He sucked in deep breaths.

"Slow down, Will," said Pa. "Are you sure it was Indians?"

"Yes, sir." Will coughed from the dusty air. He swiped his shirt sleeve across his face, smearing the dirt. "I know an Indian when I see one. He had feathers in his hair. He looked mean, real mean!"

"Was it just one?"

"Yes."

Pa and Will, with Buck following close behind, walked away from the ranch yard and up a low rise. He studied the prairie near the house, then moved his gaze farther and farther out. Will knew no clump of brush, no tree, no swell of a hill would escape Pa's careful study.

Satisfied, he turned to Will. "I don't see anything out of place, now. But we'll keep a look out."

They headed back toward the yard with Buck at their heels.

"Walk Buck to cool him down. He's sweatin'. Then let him drink. We'll put him in the barn tonight."

"Remember that white boy the Comanche stole last year? Nobody has seen him since. Do you think the Indian I saw was a Comanche?" The word "Comanche" sent arrows of fear shooting through him, pinning his feet to the ground.

"I don't know, son. I didn't see him." Pa put his hand on Will's shoulder. "Go walk Buck, but keep close. When you're finished, we'll put all the horses in the barn and pitch them some hay. I'll keep a watch tonight, and you know Buck will raise a ruckus if Indians are around."

Will pushed his fear to the pit of his stomach where that sick tobacco feeling lurked and walked Buck back and forth between the house and the barn, keeping Pa in sight. When Buck cooled down, he took him to the water trough. His hand on Buck's neck, he watched as the tall horse sucked in the cool water.

"Do you remember that boy I told you about? The one from Fredericksburg the Comanche stole? He'd be eleven now, just like me." Will rubbed his sick stomach and scooped a handful of water from the trough into his dry mouth.

"Will," Pa called as he swung the heavy barn door open. "That's enough water. Bring him on in."

Will took a deep breath, and the sickness in his stomach eased a little. He walked Buck into the barn. The cooler air smelled of cut hay.

"Your job is over when the drive is finished, right?" Will led Buck into his stall and scratched him behind his ears. "Then, when we come home, we'll have to go through Co-manche country by ourselves, won't we?"

Pa stopped working. He took a deep breath. "We are not coming back." His voice had that I've-told-you-a-million-times tone.

Will stood in the stall beside Buck. He picked up a long piece of hay from the feed trough and slipped it between his teeth. Head down, he moved closer to Buck.

"Pa, I don't want to go to New Mexico. I don't want to go through Comanche country. I don't want to get captured by the Comanche, like that other boy."

Pa propped his hayfork against the wall and put his hands on Will's shoulders. Will felt the calluses through his shirt. Somehow, the roughness reassured him.

"We'll be traveling with twenty-five hundred head of cattle and lots of drovers. When Mr. Goodnight and I were with the Texas Rangers, we learned a lot about the Comanche. We fought lots of Indians. We know the Comanche. You'll be safe."

Will followed Pa out of the barn, jamming his hands into his pockets. He hunched his shoulders and watched Pa walk toward the cabin.

"What about Ma? How can you just go off and leave her here?"

Pa stopped and turned back. His face softened. "Your mother and I talked about this many times. We thought we could make a better life in New Mexico. You have to understand, Will, Texas is ruined."

"I don't care about Texas!" Furious and frustrated, he flung his words at Pa.

Will ran back to the barn and Buck, knowing any hope of changing Pa's mind was buried in the grave with his mother.

TWO FEATHERS

Two Feathers stood behind the trunk of a sycamore just below the edge of the creek bed. He could feel his blood spurting through his arms and legs, making them twitch, pulse, and want to move. Standing still was not an easy thing to do that morning. He waited.

The birds twittered in the trees, disturbed by his presence. The morning held no hint of summer haze. It seemed he could see every detail of every blade of grass. There seemed no end to the distance. He eased his way from the creek bed up a small rise and bellied down to get a better view of the activity at the ranch.

The white man and the boy had been easy to follow. The big horse had left deep tracks. He watched the yellow-horse-with-black-mane-and-tail, a dunnia. Even from this distance, he knew he had not been wrong when he had first seen the horse earlier that morning. *How can a white boy, younger than my own twelve summers, ride such a horse? No white boy can ride like a Comanche.*

"A warrior's horse," he whispered in awe. His head swam from the sight of the magnificent stallion. *So big. So strong. So fast.*

He dreamed of riding the big horse into his village, the other boys watching in envy as he brushed the golden coat and braided his eagle feathers in the long, flowing black mane.

The morning sun brought new plans, new confidence. *I will follow the boy who rides the dunnia. My chance will come. That horse will be mine.*

Two Feathers watched as a dark-gray horse and rider burst from the pen and raced across the prairie. The boy and the dunnia followed, easily keeping pace. His heart swelled with pride. *No horse can beat you. You run fast, like the antelope.* He slipped from the crest of the hill and ran to Old Pony, leaped astride, and took off through the woods, keeping the running horses in sight. Following a gully, he reached the creek bed in time to see the gray horse with his rider leap off the bluff. It was all he could do not to let out a wild whoop in surprise. The man and horse scrambled up the other side and raced off.

Wild, like a gray wolf, fierce and strong. He, too, is a warrior's horse.

He stepped Old Pony from the cover of the trees in his amazement. Realizing his mistake, he ducked back in the shadows.

He looked across the prairie. No horse stood on the bluff. *The dunnia?* His breath caught in his throat. *Has he, too, gone over the edge?* Eyes searched the prairie and relief made him weak when he spotted horse and boy racing back to the ranch.

Two Feathers searched for the gray horse. It had disappeared over the crest of a hill. Its gutsy spirit thrilled him. *Two warrior's horses!* He sat still, lost in dreams. Old Pony nudged his shoulder. Two Feathers thoughts returned to the white man's ranch and the dunnia. *I will have you.*

He rode back down the trail and followed a deer path through the scrub oaks alongside the creek till it made a bend, and he was out of sight of the ranch. Old Pony stepped carefully down the short bank to the muddy water and drank. Two Feathers slipped from the bony back and rested his head on the rough hair of the horse's neck. He scratched under the mane and behind the scarred ears.

"You are my old friend and my father's before me. A new horse will not change that." Water dripped from Old Pony's wet muzzle as he lifted his head. The horse shifted his weight and leaned into Two Feathers. They stood in silence, comfortable in each other's presence. A quail called, "bob-white, bob-white."

A picture of the yellow-horse-with-black-mane-and-tail formed behind Two Feathers's closed eyes. *The men of the village will honor me when I take such a horse. That is the Comanche way. A warrior's horse. No one will mock me then.*

Two Feathers mounted his pony and rode toward his camp, hidden behind a white man's burial ground in some low hills several miles from the herd. He thought of the tall man and the boy who rode the dunnia—so like Two Feathers and his own father when they rode together five summers ago before the day of death. His father, too, was tall, with bright-blue eyes that crinkled at the corners when he laughed. His mother's black eyes sparkled in the evening firelight as she told them stories of her Comanche people. Sadness seeped through him as old, forgotten memories crawled their way into his mind.

Old Pony set the pace, and Two Feathers dreamed in the saddle, following the afternoon sun and leaving the miles behind him. The plains horse knew its way and stopped in the clump of trees where they had spent the previous night.

"I think we better go back to our people. I know you are tired." His words fell from his lips like worn-out leaves before winter's sleep. He slid to the ground and leaned against his old friend till he could trust the strength in his legs. "I don't want Yellow Hawk to come looking for us. He would be angry. I will tell him of the dunnia. Maybe, for once, he will be proud that I have found such a horse. Then we will come here again."

The next morning, after eating the last of the rabbit from the night before, he packed his belongings. Old Pony stood with his head down as Two Feathers tied his bundle behind the simple saddle, consisting of a pad with short stirrups.

"You can rest and grow fat on grass when the dunnia is mine."

Old Pony bobbed his head.

Two Feathers laughed. "You like that?" He swung his leg over the saddle, and they headed past the burial ground.

Two Feathers couldn't believe his luck. There was the white boy, and the dunnia! He slid off Old Pony and raced toward him, leaping over grave markers.

The white boy beat him to the dunnia, leaped astride and rode off. Two Feathers stood still and watched the dust swirl in the air. *How could such a little white boy outrun me?*

On the third day, Two Feathers rode into the village. Tepees, made of buffalo skins stretched over long poles, followed the winding banks of a creek. The reds and oranges, browns and blacks, of the figures and designs painted on them shone in the sun. Racks of buffalo meat cut into strips hung drying in the hot summer air, and smoke from cook fires drifted on the breeze. Dogs barked. Children ran to see who had arrived. He slipped off Old Pony at Yellow Hawk's tepee, where he found his aunt, Weeping Woman, scraping a deer hide staked to the ground.

She stood from her work and walked to meet him, her face shining. "You have been gone many suns. I have worried." She gave one of his braids a tug. "I am glad you are safe. But your uncle will not be happy to see you have brought no meat. It is a poor hunter who returns with nothing."

"I found a horse. A dunnia that is better than all of my uncle's horses. When I take him, Yellow Hawk will see that a white father does not keep me from being a warrior."

"Yellow Hawk is angry that you went away alone," said Weeping Woman. "You are only twelve summers. He has told you before, that is too young to be gone so long. Take your pony to the field to graze. Maybe news of this horse will soothe your uncle's anger and make him forget you brought no meat."

Two Feathers led his pony to the meadow where the village herd grazed. He removed the hackamore from the horse's head and smiled as his old friend trotted out to the herd.

"You have been gone many suns. Did you ride that old pony, or did you have to carry him?" Barks Like Coyote said as he leaned against a cottonwood tree.

Two Feathers glared at the older boy. "Guard the herd." His voice was low and hard. "I found a better horse than any man in the village." His back stiff with anger, Two Feathers walked away, ignoring the sneering laughter.

He returned to his uncle's tepee. His steps slowed as he saw Yellow Hawk talking to Weeping Woman. As she spoke to her husband, she put her hand on his arm. Yellow Hawk knocked it off, turned from her, and stalked away. She picked up the buffalo bone scraper and continued her work on the deer hide. Two Feathers sat beside her.

"Stay away from Yellow Hawk for a time," she told him. "He does not believe you saw the horse you speak of. Let his anger cool. He killed a deer, so we have meat to eat. Get me some buffalo chips for the fire and water."

Two Feathers did not go. He picked up a stick and drew horses in the dirt. He snuck a quick glance at Weeping Woman. "Yellow Hawk does not know. I have seen it. There is such a horse."

Weeping Woman tugged his braid again, a habit she'd learned from the boy's mother. "I believe you speak the truth. Now, go. The fire will soon die down."

Two Feathers frowned at the task but picked up baskets and a water pouch and headed for the woods. As he passed the last tepee, Red Wing came up and walked alongside him.

"Where are you going, Two Feathers?"

He turned to her and gulped. "To get buffalo chips and water for Weeping Woman." For some reason, his voice always squeaked when she was near.

"I will go with you." Red Wing took his hand, and they left the village. "You were gone many suns. I was worried. Your pony is old. I feared something had happened to him."

Two Feathers did not know how to get his hand loose— maybe he wasn't so sure he wanted it loose. "No, he is fine." He stopped and turned to her. He could not keep the excitement from his face.

"I found a warrior's horse. A big dunnia. Strong enough for a war chief to ride into battle. Someday I will . . . " He stopped. A group of young boys galloped up in a swirl of dust.

"Two Feathers, where is this horse you spoke of? We want to race," laughed Barks Like Coyote. "Does he look like your old pony? This time, we will walk our horses. Maybe, that way, you can win." The boys laughed as they rode on.

Two Feathers stomped off toward the creek. When he knelt to fill the pouch, his knee landed on a sharp stone. "Ow!" he yelled as a drop of blood trickled down his leg. Rising, he kicked the rock into the water. He tied the bag, slung the strap over his shoulder, and grabbed the baskets.

Red Wing followed him out onto the prairie to hunt for buffalo chips. "Barks Like Coyote is mean. Do not listen to him."

Two Feathers turned to her. "Soon, I will have that horse. I have seen him at the camp of the whites." He leaned over to pick up the dried chips and put them in a basket.

"You must not go there. The whites will kill you." Her voice trembled. She reached for his hand again.

He looked at Red Wing with her black hair tucked behind her ears—her soft black eyes shining up at him, her smooth skin that he suddenly wanted so much to touch. What had happened to the little girl with the dirty face and tangled hair that used to follow him everywhere?

"Don't worry. I have no fear of whites. Someday, I will race the buffalo across the flat land on my dunnia. I will be a great warrior. Yellow Hawk and Barks Like Coyote will follow me into battle."

Red Wing dumped all her chips into his basket.

When the baskets were full, Two Feathers gave Red Wing one of them. They returned to the village. He watched her walk to her mother, and he waved.

At Yellow Hawk's tepee, he placed the buffalo chips near the fire and then laid the pouch of water beside Weeping Woman. The chief sat in the shade of the tepee, braiding a long riata from buffalo hide strips. His legs, covered with soft deerskin moccasins to his hips, stretched before him. He watched Two Feathers.

"Picking up chips is women's work. Are you a woman?"

Two Feathers looked at the hard lines of the man's face. His heart caught in his chest. He held his breath. "I have found a horse." The words exploded with a gush of air.

"Weeping Woman told me. You have the worst horse of all the young men. How would you know a good horse? Your horse is old and weak. You should have killed it long ago."

Two Feathers rushed at Yellow Hawk. "No more." His voice was sharp and hard like arrowheads. "Stop speaking so about the horse my father gave me!"

Yellow Hawk leaped to his feet, his face dark with anger. He stepped close to Two Feathers. His hatred for the white man roared out of him like stampeding buffalo. "If you were not the son of my sister, I would kill you." He grabbed Two Feathers by the neck and choked him. "I would kill you as I killed your white traitor father."

"No!" cried Weeping Woman. "Yellow Hawk, no!" She jumped to her feet and ran to Two Feathers.

Heads turned. Several men and women hurried in their direction.

His face fierce, Yellow Hawk threw the boy to the ground, pushed through the watching people, and stalked away.

Two Feathers gasped for air and clutched his aching throat. His eyes bulged. He sat up and looked at Weeping Woman. "Is that true?" he gasped. "Did Yellow Hawk kill my father?"

Weeping Woman brought him water to drink. The sadness in her eyes told Two Feathers the truth of his uncle's words. "He believes your father brought the soldiers that raided our camp that day, who killed your mother and so many of our people."

"No!" he cried. "My father would never do such a thing." He scrambled to his feet and stretched out his arm toward Yellow Hawk's retreating back, fist clenched in defiance and rage. In a hoarse croak, he shouted, "You killed my father. I will live with you no more." He ran from the village, far out onto the empty open prairie.

When darkness came, Two Feathers waited until clouds dimmed the light of the moon. He slipped from the shadows into Yellow Hawk's tepee. He listened for any change in the soft snores of his uncle, but there was none. Gathering his sleeping skins, his bow, and his quiver of arrows, he stepped toward the man wrapped in blankets, a knife in his fist. *You are no longer my mother's brother. You are no longer my uncle. You are not my family.*

Weeping Woman raised her head. The tears in her eyes shone in the glow of the fire's coals. He looked at her, then at his knife, and slipped it back in its sheath. She nodded toward a bundle beside the open flap of the tepee, then lay back down and turned away. Her soft sobs wrenched a hole in his heart.

Two Feathers grabbed the bundle and slipped from the tepee. Mounting Old Pony, he rode into the night. His hatred for Yellow Hawk and his desire for the dunnia burned like hot coals. Jaws clenched in hatred for his uncle and a heart heavy with sorrow for Weeping Woman and Red Wing, he rode away from the only home he had known since the day of death.

I am Comanche, and I am white. The Comanche will take the dunnia. The white will kill Yellow Hawk.

THE DRIVE

No home.

Will lay on the hard ground, wrapped in a scratchy wool blanket. His back hurt.

Not even a barn for Buck.

He pulled the cover over his head. Something sharp under his ground cloth jabbed his hip. He squirmed and wiggled to find a smooth spot.

He missed his bed on the ranch and the soft nightshirt his mother had made. The cowboys slept in their clothes, so he'd left his nightshirt packed in the wagon. He didn't want to look like a kid.

It grew hot under the cover. He pulled it off his head and breathed in the cool air. A faint glow peeked above the horizon in the eastern sky. Last night, in his eagerness at spending his first day on a trail drive, he'd forgotten about leaving home and his mother. The sound of the cattle as they settled in for the night, an occasional cough, the clacking of horns as they bumped each other, the lowing of a mother for her calf, had fueled his excitement and held sleep at bay. Finally, the flickering light of the fire had lulled him to sleep.

He rubbed his eyes and thought about the last week. Closing out their ranch had been hard. He argued with Pa every time they were together. Packing his mother's things and sending them to her family back East had chased all thoughts of the drive away. Again, he pulled the blanket over his head as he remembered the harsh words he had spoken to Pa about sending Ma's rocking chair. Will remembered her rocking and softly singing as she sewed. He rolled over and buried his face in the crook of his arm. He didn't remember the words he had yelled, but he knew they were awful.

Pa had said to pick something small he could remember her by. He had carefully rolled her favorite green hair ribbon into a tight roll. He worked his fingers into his pocket. It was still there.

Will poked his head from under his blanket and watched Cookie stir the coals in the campfire. The short, stocky man added wood. A flame blazed up. Light spilled over him, showing his shaggy beard and gnarled hands. He put the coffee pot on the fire and limped to the rear of the chuck wagon. From a bin, he scooped several double handfuls of flour into a large wooden mixing bowl, adding some lard, baking powder, salt, and water. He stirred and scraped the sides of the bowl and dumped the dough onto the table that hung from the back of the wagon. Will's mouth watered as he thought of Cookie's tall, golden biscuits dripping with honey from last night's supper. He watched Mr. Goodnight walk to the coffee pot and pour a cup of the steaming brew. The shadow their tall trail boss cast from the fire seemed to reach out to Will.

"Roust the boys out, Cookie," Goodnight said as he sipped his coffee. "We'll start the herd today. Pack the chuck wagon after breakfast and head southwest. Take the old Butterfield stage route toward Camp Cooper." He turned to walk off. "Keep a sharp lookout," he said and stared toward the distant hills. "I'm sure I saw a wisp of smoke last night to the west of us. It could be Comanche."

Comanche! Will ducked his head back under the covers. His heart banged into the back of his throat, cutting off his breath. *Maybe Mr. Goodnight knows if anyone ever found that boy they took.* He felt sick and rubbed his belly. Slipping his hand into his pocket, he touched the green ribbon. *I hope Pa is right, and he and Mr. Goodnight can fight Indians.*

Will lay curled in his blanket and listened to the sounds of morning on a cattle drive—pots banging, bacon sizzling, cowboys grumbling as they rose from their blankets, stretched, and stomped into their boots. His heart slowed and settled into its normal place. He sucked in a deep breath.

"Come and get it before I throw it out!" Cookie hollered as he dished up beans, bacon, and biscuits.

Will kicked off his blanket, yawned, and stretched. He shook his boots to empty out any crawling critters and shoved his feet into them. His hand ran through his hair, smoothing it down enough to put on his hat. Pushing through sleepy drovers to stand next to Pa by the fire, he held out a cup so Cookie could fill it. Will took a careful sip. The strong, bitter coffee scalded his tongue and stung his throat.

Pa handed him a plate and grinned. "The older you get, the better it tastes."

"It's time we head this herd for Buffalo Gap," Mr. Goodnight announced to the men. He popped the last of his biscuit in his mouth and tossed his plate in the wash bucket. "I made arrangements for Rich Coffee to meet us there with more horses in about ten days. Sittin' around eating Cookie's biscuits ain't gettin' us to New Mexico. Saddle up. I'll meet you at the remuda to make riding assignments."

The men whooped and hollered. Caught up in their excitement, Will yelled, "Yee-haw!" He gobbled the last few bites, tossed his plate and cup in the wash bucket, and took off for the remuda.

"Whoa, there," Pa said as he grabbed the back of Will's shirt. "Hold on a minute. A drover takes care of his belongings. He doesn't leave them for others to pick up. Roll your blankets and put them in the chuck wagon. No one has time to wait on you."

Will pulled away from his grasp and quickly rolled his blankets. When he stood, Pa was waiting for him.

"Are you feeling better? Today is a big day."

Will remembered he was mad at Pa and shrugged. The excitement of starting the drive was too strong for his anger. He grinned. "You bet I am."

"I have a goin' away present for you." Pa headed for the wagon. "Let's see if it fits. Cookie, where's that box I asked you to hide for me?"

"Look behind that stack of flour sacks."

Pa climbed into the chuck wagon and came out with a large round box. The night drovers coming into camp gathered around to see, smiles on their faces.

"You got me a present?" Will ducked his head and stirred the dirt with the toe of his boot, trying to hide his excitement. "It's not my birthday."

"I know. But it's something you need for the drive."

Will lifted the lid and pulled out a new brown felt cowboy hat. "Thanks, Pa," he mumbled, taking off his old worn hat and placing the new one carefully on his head. He wiggled it around until he found just the right spot. "It fits." The corner of his mouth twitched, and a big smile broke out.

"Put the old one in the box and take care of this one," said Pa. "We'll shape it tonight when we make camp. A good hat is important on a cattle drive."

Pa picked up their saddles. Will put the hatbox with his old hat back behind the flour sacks and grabbed the bridles. They headed for the remuda, not too far from camp.

Naldo, the bowlegged, wiry horse wrangler, led Buck from the rope corral, saddled him, and gave Will a boost up. "Be careful out there today. Those cattle muy loco."

"I know, Naldo. See my new hat?"

Naldo grinned. "Si. Me gusta mucho. Que bonito tu sombrero. You ready to go?"

Pa and the drovers mounted their horses. Laughter mingled with the dust stirred up by the antics of half-broke horses. Guilt at leaving Ma slipped into his stomach and gave his eagerness to start a real trail drive a hefty punch. "I guess I have to be."

Will and Pa rode over to Mr. Goodnight and reined their horses next to the trail boss.

"Rory," called the boss, "take swing on the north side of the herd."

"Yes, sir." As he rode off, Rory swung his hat in a circle and plopped it back on top of his curly, black hair.

Goodnight looked over the men.

"How about Curtis on south swing," Pa recommended.

"What about me, Mr. Goodnight? Where do I go?" asked Will.

"Curtis, that's your spot," said the boss.

"See you out there, Will-boy," hollered Curtis as he followed Rory.

Will watched them ride off. *Are they just going to leave me out?* Buck sidestepped and turned in a circle, eager to go with them. "Whoa, Buck." Will pulled up the slack in the reins.

Goodnight turned to the waiting men. "Russ, you and Hank take flank on each side. Tell the boys on guard to space themselves out between you two and the swing riders."

"Where do you want me?" Will looked at Mr. Goodnight, then Pa. No one answered him. "Last week he said I was a good cowboy, and now he won't give me a job," he mumbled just loud enough for Buck to hear. He stood in the stirrups and watched the two older men ride out to take their places on each side toward the end of the herd. *Maybe he's gonna put me on drag. He said I did a good job there.*

Pa watched the two men ride off. "That's a steady pair. They've been up the trail before. If those young hotheads on swing don't tend to business, they'll catch the backside of Hank's tongue."

"What about us, boss?"

They turned to look at what appeared to be the same young man sitting on two different horses. Will blinked, not trusting his eyes. The young men had the same green eyes, the same red hair and freckles, the same hat, shirt, pants, and worn boots. The only things different about them were the horses they rode.

"I never know which one of you is Tony and which is Jake, but both of you ride drag." Goodnight glanced back and forth between the two.

"Aw, boss, drag?" asked one.

"That job's a killer," said the other.

"I'll ride drag," Will offered. "You said I was good."

"I put you boys there on purpose," Goodnight told the twins. "I've seen the two of you work drag before. There's none better. Besides, I've made a deal with Cookie. Each day there'll be a special treat after dinner for the drag riders."

Identical grins spread across identical faces. "You got a deal," said Jake as they headed toward the back end of the herd. Pa watched the two lope off and chuckled.

"What about me?" Will looked around. No more drovers waited for assignments. Only Will. No one told him where to go. *I'm a drover. I'm going to the herd. I can do anything those two can.* Frustration got the better of him, and he jerked Buck's reins and kicked him hard.

Buck turned and jumped into a gallop just as an old man dressed in buckskins rode up on a long-legged brown horse. Buck smashed into the other horse, and both animals reared on their hind legs. The old man and Will grabbed manes and saddle horns to keep their seats and struggled to control their mounts. Pa's horse and Goodnight's backed off out of range of sharp hooves.

"Buck. No!" yelled Will as he pulled hard on the reins to turn away from the confused jumble of horses and riders.

Pa reached out and grabbed Buck's reins just below the chin strap. Pulling the animal away, he yelled at Will.

"What are you doing? You know better than that."

"Sorry, Pa." Will rubbed Buck's neck to calm him down, his head drooping with embarrassment.

"One more stunt like that and you'll spend this cattle drive riding in the chuck wagon!"

The old man grinned at Pa. "Don't be too hard on the boy. This old horse of mine is so used to ridin' in Injun country, he steps mighty quiet. The boy didn't know I was here." A stub of pipe clenched in his teeth poked out through the thick, gray beard. He winked at Will.

Will held Buck as still as he could. He didn't want to cause any more trouble and get banished to the chuck wagon. He'd end up collecting firewood and hauling water the whole drive.

"Hello, Smokey." Pa turned to Goodnight. "Where did you find this old scout?"

The trail boss frowned at Will, then answered Pa. "I've been looking for him for weeks and finally found him at Fort Belknap the day I was at your place." He shook the old man's hand. "What's it look like ahead?"

"I've scouted the trail for about thirty miles and have campsites spotted. We're in good shape for water for the next few days." Smokey reached for Pa's hand. "How you doin', Dan?"

Goodnight glanced back at Will. "Maybe you better keep Will close to you for a few days till this herd gets trail broke."

"You hear that, Will?" asked Pa. "Stick close."

"No, Pa. I can—"

"No argument!"

At Pa's stern expression, Will swallowed his angry reply.

"Dan, take point on the far side. I'll take this side," said Goodnight. "We'll head the leaders southwest." He turned to Smokey. "Cookie may still have coffee and biscuits if you hurry." He and Pa headed for the herd. Will turned Buck to follow.

"Did you hear that, Buck?" Will said. "It's not fair. We can do as good a job as the other riders." He slouched in the saddle. *I didn't want to come on this drive anyway.* A backward glance from his father made him spur Buck to catch up.

"Pa, when is Mr. Goodnight gonna see I'm as good a cowboy as any of those guys?" Buck snorted and turned his ears back toward Will, as if to say *We can do anything they can do.*

"Oh, is that what you just did? Show him what a good cowboy you are?"

With his head hanging, Will glanced at Pa. The angry face kept him quiet.

After a few minutes of silence, Pa reined his horse to a stop. "I know what you can do, but this is dangerous, serious work." Pa shifted his weight in the saddle and leaned over to Will. "The men don't have time to look after you. It's not like the few hours we spent driving our cattle at the ranch. These cattle are not like the ones we had at home. Most of them have been gathered in from the wild, and like any wild animal, they'll attack you if they feel threatened. Don't wander off. The boss said to stay with me, so that's what you'll do."

"Yes, sir." He had not seen that obey-me-or-else expression in a long time.

Will followed Pa out to the herd. The noise grew louder as they neared the bedding ground. The quiet, lazy-looking cattle of the night before milled and bawled in confusion as the drovers hollered and slapped coiled lariats against their leather chaps. The startling, loud pop made the cattle lunge to their feet. Pa and Goodnight rode their horses in among the lead steers and, swinging the ends of their ropes in circles, popped their rumps with stinging flicks. The herd started toward the southwest.

Will watched Pa and soon mastered the popping motion that would move a stubborn animal in the direction he wanted it to go.

"Ho, cattle, ho, ho," called Will as he pushed and prodded the animals along. Dust filled the air. Cattle bawled, and long, pointed horns gleamed in the sunlight as the beeves turned in every direction, confused by the noise and wanting to return to their homes.

After chasing steers, cows, and calves in what Will swore was circles, he decided being a drover was the worst job he had ever done. He had dust in his teeth. His butt and legs ached. Sweat dripped from under his new hat, staining the band. Will kicked Buck after a steer, chasing it back into the herd for the third time.

He rode alongside Pa and took a drink from his canteen. "This is crazy, Pa. Is it going to be like this every day? These durn critters go every direction except the one we want them to go." He jerked his hat off, brushed the dust off it with his bandana, wiped the sweatband, and settled it back on his head.

"The first few days are always the worst." Pa drank deep from his canteen. "I told you it would be hard work. When they get trail broke, it won't be so bad."

They rode up on the top of a low swell in the prairie. Will stood in his stirrups and looked back down the trail. "I can still see where we camped last night. We'll never get to New Mexico going this slow. Are you sure this is a good idea?"

Pa didn't answer. He rode off after a small bunch of steers veering off from the herd.

Will didn't follow. He slumped in the saddle. Through the distant, dusty haze, he watched the twins riding drag and the other cowboys on flank and on swing working to squeeze the cattle into a long line. As steers broke away, riders chased them back. Dust roiled up into the air and choked his breath as the men worked to keep the herd moving. *Why are we doing this? I want to go home. I don't know what Pa is thinking.*

Finally, Will kicked Buck into a lope and caught up with Pa. They rode up and down the front-runners of the line, working to keep the lead animals headed in the right direction.

Will relaxed in the saddle for a brief few minutes when there was a lull in the number of escaping cattle. "Pa, see that big blue steer. Why's he got a bell around his neck? He's got the biggest horns I've ever seen."

"That's Ol' Blue."

"He's worked all the way to the front, like he belongs there."

"He does. He's Charlie's lead steer. Once they're trail broke, the herd will follow that clanging bell. You watch him. He'll fight any steer that tries to take his place."

The hot sun beat down. The back of Will's neck itched from the dust that worked its way down his collar. He wondered if they were ever going to stop. His backside hurt. His stomach growled continually. Breakfast seemed like a long time ago.

The water in his canteen was hot and tasted awful. He wiped sweat and dirt from his face with his bandana. *A cool drink of water would sure be good.* He licked his dry lips.

At lunch, the men changed weary horses for fresh ones. Will turned Buck over to Naldo. The buckskin lay down and rolled in the dry grass. His legs waved in the air as he squirmed to clean the sweat from his back. When he stood, he shook himself, throwing grass and dust off his coat.

Will walked over to a group of drovers standing around a horse apart from the others. When he got close, he saw a deep cut in the horse's hip. Goodnight held the horse's head, and Cookie spread thick salve on the cut.

"What happened?" Will asked Curtis.

"One of the swing riders didn't get out of the way quick enough. An ol' mossy-horned steer raked that bay."

Will walked with Curtis to the cook fire. The sight of that bloody gash lingered and stole his appetite. They filled their plates with beef stew and leaned against the wagon wheel to eat in silence for several minutes. Curtis wolfed his down, but Will picked at the stew and stirred it around in his plate.

"You be careful out there, Will-boy." Curtis mopped up the last of his stew with a biscuit. "These old steers that have been wild all their lives can turn quick. They'll gut you if they get a chance."

Will's stomach flopped around. He didn't want Buck to end up like that bay. The stew didn't look so good anymore. He gave his plate to Curtis. "Here, eat mine. I'm not hungry."

"Will," Pa called. "Mount up. Let's go."

The long, hot hours of the afternoon passed slowly. Will's new respect for the sharp horns of the brush cattle kept his attention focused on his job. He decided, if Buck was going to be safe, he'd better learn how to be a good drover.

"Pa, don't you think Buck is rested enough? I don't like this horse," Will said after a few hours on the strange mount.

"I guess so. See the remuda off to the right?"

Will nodded and spurred the horse in his eagerness to find Buck.

The sun hung low in the western sky before Pa and Goodnight turned the herd toward the spot Smokey had picked for the night camp. A good-sized creek wound its way through scattered clusters of cottonwood trees. Buck bent his head to drink. Will's throat was dry, but he didn't like the look of the muddy water along the bank. He decided to wait till he returned to camp.

He looked down the trail at the line of cattle stretched as far as he could see. Pa rode up and stopped to let his horse drink. Will and Pa sat in their saddles as the sky turned gold, then purple and pink.

"Pa," Will said, pointing back the way they'd come, "it looks like a river of cattle."

"A river of cattle?" Pa wiped sweat from his face. "A good name for what we're pushing. A river that's as smooth as well water through a trough, but sometimes explodes like a waterfall down a rocky cliff."

BUFFALO GAP

Rory sang as he and Will rode a lazy circle around the herd. The stars winked in the sky, and the cattle settled in for the night. Most of them had lain down, but some remained restless, still on their feet and grazing.

"Oh, bury me not on the lone prairie.
These words came low and mournfully
From the pallid lips of a youth who lay
On his dying bed at the close of day."

Rory's mellow tenor floated on the night breeze and blended with the soft lowing of a cow for her calf. Clouds drifted away, and the moon bathed the cattle in a soft light.

"Oh, bury me not on the lone prairie,
Where the coyotes howl and the wind blows free.
In a narrow grave just six by three,
Oh, bury me not on the lone prairie."

"Why do cowboys always sing such sad songs when you ride night herd?" Will eased himself in the saddle.

"I guess 'cause it's soothin'. If you want cattle, or young'uns for that matter, to go to sleep, you sing 'em a lullaby, not a toe-tappin' dance tune."

Curtis came riding up from the other side of the herd. "How's everything over here?" he asked.

"Things seem pretty quiet tonight," said Rory.

"Will-boy, Dan said for you to come back to camp pretty quick," said Curtis. He flipped up the back of Will's new hat.

"Quit that." Catching his hat, he set it back on his head. "You better not ruin my new hat."

"Get back to camp," Curtis warned, swiping at his hat again. "You don't want your Pa to come huntin' you."

Will rode into camp, pulled the saddle off, and turned Buck into the rope corral.

"How's it goin' out there?" Pa picked up Will's heavy saddle and dropped it not far from his own. He stretched out on his blankets.

"Quiet." Will spread his blankets and leaned against his saddle. A cool breeze dried the sweat from his face. He searched for the Big Dipper and found it. The cup was tilted up.

He remembered Ma used to tell stories about explorers tramping across the sky searching for water. If they found the Big Dipper in the wee hours of the morning, the cup would hold water. They could drink their fill. But if they found it in the early hours of the night, the cup would be tipped over, and all the water would spill out onto the Earth. They would go thirsty. Ma believed in always carrying water everywhere you went. He slipped his hand into his pocket and found the green ribbon.

A pack of coyotes' high yipping barks interrupted his thoughts. The howling serenade ended with their mournful cries. He sat up. Cookie walked between the fire and the wagon. His shadow and those of the men moving around camp passed across the canvas wagon cover. He slid further down so only his head rested on his saddle and rolled in his blanket.

"Grub's on, boys." Cookie's call to breakfast dragged Will from his sleep. "The sun won't wait for a lazy lot of loafers. The last one to the coffee pot gets the grounds." Cookie poured Mr. Goodnight the first cup.

Will shook out his boots, crammed his feet into them, plopped his newly shaped hat on his head, and rolled his blanket. He gobbled his bacon and biscuits and let Curtis pour coffee into his cup. Even though he took a small sip of the hot coffee, it burned his tongue. He walked to the men talking near the supply wagon.

"We'll make Buffalo Gap by late afternoon," Mr. Goodnight said. "Rich Coffee is meeting us there with horses from his Flat Top Ranch at Picketville. Dan and I'll ride on ahead and look them over."

Naldo led the grullo for the trail boss and Pa's sorrel from the remuda. Both men mounted, and Goodnight headed south.

"Will," Pa called, his horse prancing in a circle, eager to be off. "Stay with Curtis and Rory today. Don't wander off."

"Pa. Wait!" Will yelled.

Pebbles flew from the horse's hooves as it sprang into a gallop after Goodnight. All he could see was the back end of the horse as Pa rode away.

"I don't want to ride with Curtis." Will kicked his foot at a rock. It skipped across camp and smacked into Curtis's boot.

"Hey, there. Don't cripple your ridin' partner." Curtis tried to flip Will's hat, but Will jumped out of reach.

Will finished his breakfast and followed the men to the rope corral. He realized this would be the first day he could ride with the other drovers without Pa around. *Maybe today they'll see I know what I'm doing and stop treating me like a kid.* He felt better and wanted to start the drive.

The men saddled their horses and headed for the herd. Curtis threw the heavy saddle on Buck and cinched it tight. He cupped his hands to give Will a boost. Will eyed him warily.

"Don't you trust me, Will-boy?" asked Curtis with a grin.

"No shenanigans, Curtis. We have work to do, remember?"

"You can trust me," he said as Will slipped his boot into the tough-skinned hands that tossed him aboard the tall buckskin.

Will grabbed Curtis's hat, and—waving it in a circle overhead—he raced toward the herd. "Catch me, Curtis-boy, and I'll give your hat back."

"Come back here!" Curtis raced for his Appaloosa.

"If that ol' nag of yours can't catch Buck, I'm gonna feed your hat to some ol' mossy-horned steer."

Curtis's spotted horse jumped into a full gallop before he even got his leg over the saddle.

Will sat with one leg around the saddle horn, twirling the hat, as Curtis rode up. "About time you got here. We got work to do." He tossed the hat to the cowboy.

"You got me that time, Will-boy. You sure did."

Will, Curtis, and Rory took up their position on flank. Cowboys whooped and hollered, popped their lariats on their chaps, and the animals lunged to their feet. Ol' Blue took the lead, and the river of cattle flowed toward the Gap. Will trailed behind Curtis and in front of Rory. Moving at an easy pace, the longhorns stopped to graze as they followed the ones moving ahead of them.

The sun rose from its bed of orange clouds and poured the August heat down on the already scorched prairie. Will tapped Buck into a lope, caught up with Curtis, and rode alongside him for a while.

"They sure are easy to handle this morning," he said.

"Don't complain. These critters are notional. They might get it in their heads to take off in any direction at any moment."

"How come just a few days ago we were fighting them all the time to keep them going in one direction? Now they walk along together like they been doin' it forever."

"Cattle get used to doing things one way, and they don't like to change." He grinned at Will. "Kind of like some folks I know."

"Who are you talking about?"

Curtis laughed and veered his horse slightly to turn a calf back toward its mother. "After a while, they get used to the new way and are happy with it. They like being with each other. Kind of like making friends, I guess. That's why a herd stays together. They like the company."

After a few hours of slow going to let the cattle graze, Rory hollered at Curtis to pick up the pace. Will moved up and down the line, keeping the cattle moving through the late morning. Pride at the job he was doing settled in him. He knew he was a good cowhand and wanted the others to know it too. *I'm not goin' to hang around Pa like a suckling calf. Buck and I know what we're doin'.*

Earlier, the cattle had spread out to graze, but now he watched Curtis, Rory, and the other drovers pushing them tighter, narrowing the line until it was about eight to ten abreast.

Nothing got past Will and Buck as they worked between Curtis and Rory. The cattle soon settled in at the new pace, and the line stretched out as far as Will could see in front and behind him.

"Is Buffalo Gap a town?" he asked Curtis as they rode alongside the herd.

Curtis swung the end of his rope and popped a lazy steer, encouraging him to catch up. "No, it's an old buffalo trail through a break in the hills. There's grass there and good water. It's a camping spot the Indians and Mexican traders have used for years." Curtis looked at Rory, who rode up from his flank position behind them. "But there's a big hotel there, the Elm Hotel."

"A hotel? But you said it wasn't a town," said Will.

"It sounds strange, don't it?" Rory grinned. He spun his horse after a wayward steer.

The sun seemed to stand still in the sky as Will and the drovers poked, prodded, and pushed the cattle southwest toward Buffalo Gap. Sweat trickled down Will's face as he worked between Rory and Curtis. Thoughts of a soft hotel bed occupied his mind through the long, hot afternoon.

"Look ahead a ways, Will-boy," said Curtis. He and Will stopped to mop the dust off the backs of their necks. "See that opening in the hills?" He stretched his arm toward the horizon. "That's Buffalo Gap. There's grass aplenty, and Elm Creek flows cool and sweet."

"How long till we get there? Can we swim? I sure am hot."

"Won't be long." The dusty cowboy spurred his horse after a steer spending too much time savoring a clump of grass.

As the afternoon shadows grew longer, Will pushed the same cow and her calf back into the herd once again when the twins, Tony and Jake, came riding up to relieve them.

"Howdy, Jake," Will called. "Did you see the hotel?"

"I'm Tony. What hotel? There's a good-sized swimming spot in the creek. I can't wait to jump in. Mr. Coffee brought his boy with him. Looks to be about your age. Dan said to come a-runnin'. He wants you to say howdy."

Will looked at Rory, then at Curtis. Merriment danced on their faces. "What's so funny? How come, when I ask about this hotel, no one knows what I'm talking about? If we're gonna sleep in it, how come Cookie's making camp?" Will narrowed his eyes. "You better not be funnin' me again."

"Come on, let's go swimming." Rory whooped and took off for camp in the Gap.

Curtis spurred his horse and left Will and Buck standing in a swirl of dust.

"Buck, I don't trust them. Something's just not right." With a kick from Will, Buck leaped into a full gallop and caught, then passed, the two riders.

They raced up to camp with Buck in the lead. The men scattered as Buck slid to a stop, kicking up dust. Will bailed off and ran to Pa, standing with a group of men, each holding a cup of steaming coffee.

"Will, what the heck are you doing?" yelled Pa. He grabbed Buck's reins, dropping his coffee cup, but stopping the big horse. "What's wrong? You know better than to ride into camp like that."

"Sorry, Pa," said Will. "When are we going to the hotel? A bed sure will feel good. We're going to stay in Buffalo Gap tonight, aren't we?"

"Hotel? What are you talking about, boy?" asked a burly, long-haired man, who checked his coffee for dirt before taking another sip.

"The Elm Hotel," answered Curtis with a wink. "The place where all the trappers stay when they come through here."

Charlie Goodnight looked around the fire at the men's grinning faces. "The Elm Hotel? Oh, yes. I'd forgotten about that."

"Can we, Pa? Is there a hotel? Can we sleep in a real bed tonight?"

Pa looked around the circle of men, smiles hidden behind cups of coffee.

"Umm—hotel?" He took a long sip of his coffee.

Curtis cleared his throat.

"Sure, son. We're all going to stay at the Elm Hotel tonight," Pa said.

A bark of laughter burst from a tall boy stepping from behind the burly man.

"Will," said Pa, "this is Mr. Rich Coffee and his son, Bill. You boys unsaddle Buck and turn him over to Naldo. Then you can go swimming before supper."

Will took Buck's reins. *What's going on here? I don't see any hotel.* He looked at Curtis. The man turned his head away, but not before Will spotted the mischief on his face.

"Will," Pa said again, "I said take Buck to Naldo."

Will walked away from the group of men. *No hotel! No bed, either. Just more hard ground. Why'd Pa go along with their joke? Sometimes I just don't get Pa.*

Will lifted his chin and drew in a slow breath.

"Come on, Bill." His face felt hot, and he knew it was red. "Can you swim?"

"'Course I can. You aren't dumb enough to believe that about a hotel?"

That boy better hobble his lip, or I'm gonna knock that grin off his face.

"This ain't nothin' but a camping spot." Bill stepped close to Will and, being a head and shoulders taller, looked down at him. "That big elm tree over there is called the Elm Hotel 'cause everyone stops here when they come through the Gap. We stay here every time we go to the Pecos to get wagonloads of salt."

Will stopped. He looked up at Bill and rubbed at the dirt with the toe of his boot. *You big saphead.* "Naw, I knew they were funnin'."

The next morning, Will stood at the breakfast fire and glared across at Bill. *If one more cowboy asks me how I liked sleepin' in a hotel bed, I'm gonna bust.* He watched Bill slip behind his father and mimic sleeping in a bed.

Rich Coffee set his cup by the coffeepot. "Ok, Bill, let's head for home."

Father and son followed Pa, Will, and Mr. Goodnight to the remuda. Naldo handed the reins of a fine-looking black horse to Mr. Coffee and a pinto to Bill. Buck nudged Will, causing him to stumble, and Mr. Coffee chuckled.

"Goodnight, that's a mighty fine buckskin stallion there," he said. "I've got some mares at home I'd like to put with him. What will you take for him?"

Will looked at Naldo and rolled his eyes. The wrangler boosted Will into the saddle.

Bill's mouth dropped open. "How's that boy gonna ride that stallion? He can't even mount by himself."

Mr. Coffee walked to Buck and ran his hand down the horse's flank.

Buck snorted and laid his ears flat against his head. He sidestepped away from the man's touch.

"Buck is mine." Will stroked the tense muscled neck.

"Yours?" Mr. Coffee laughed and turned to Goodnight. "Charlie?"

"He's Will's."

"That horse can't belong to this skinny boy." Bill walked up beside his pa. "He's too little to climb in the saddle. He needs a pony."

"And you're too dumb to know anything. Get away from my horse." Will felt the rush of blood in his face.

"Take it easy," warned Pa.

Will glared at him, remembering his part in the joke about the hotel.

Rich Coffee looked from one boy to the other. "Bill, remember we're guests here. You boys go back to camp and get the supplies Cookie packed for us."

Will reined Buck around and headed toward camp, not waiting for Bill to mount.

When Bill caught up, his pinto seemed to shrink beside the big stallion. "How'd you get a horse like this?"

"Buck and I have always been together."

"Ha! I saw the wrangler boost you in the saddle. You're so little, I bet you can't mount him without help."

Will reined Buck to a stop and sat still for a minute. The corners of his mouth twitched. He struggled to keep his face blank. "I'll take that bet. What are you gonna ante up?"

"I got a big bag of rock candy. You?"

"My pocketknife."

"Against a bag of candy?" Bill's eyes popped, and his voice squeaked.

Without a word, Will stuck out his hand. Bill grabbed it, and the boys shook, sealing the bet. Will stood in his stirrups and looked around. He spotted a cluster of willow trees along the creek. "Follow me."

The boys rode through the trees to a clearing out of sight of camp and dismounted.

"Okay." Bill's sneer fed Will's satisfaction. "Get on him. There's nothing here to climb on and no one to give you a boost. Is that pocketknife real sharp? I sure do like a sharp knife."

"And I sure do like rock candy."

He grabbed both reins in his left hand just below the chin-strap and pulled Buck's head down. Reaching out with his right, he tapped the stallion's knees. "Down, boy, down." Buck bent his front legs and went to his knees. Will tossed the reins over the horse's head. The left stirrup now within reach, Will slipped his boot into it and swung his right leg over the saddle as Buck scrambled back to his feet.

Bill stared first at Buck, then up at Will. "How'd you ever get him to do that? I ain't never saw a horse do that before."

Will leaned down from the saddle into Bill's face. "Listen, you blowhard, I'm no tenderfoot caught between hay and grass. I may be little, but Buck and I take care of each other. I don't ask him to do that often because I don't want his knees scratched up. Pay up!"

With all the good-byes said, Will, Pa, and Goodnight watched as father and son rode from camp. They hadn't gone far when Mr. Coffee reined his horse to a halt and turned to Bill.

"I wonder why they're stopping," Pa said.

"Do you think they forgot something?" Charlie shaded his eyes with his hat to see better.

Just then, they heard a booming laugh. Rich Coffee spurred his horse and took off at a gallop. Bill slowly followed.

For once, I came out on top. I put the joke on someone else. Will busted out laughing

Pa and Charlie looked at him.

"What's so funny?" Pa asked.

"You'll see after dinner. I have a surprise for everyone."

That night, everyone in camp had a piece of rock candy for dessert. The drag riders had two. Will's story of how he came to have rock candy grew with each telling as the hungry drovers rotated into camp for supper.

ALONE

Leaving Yellow Hawk's village, Two Feathers rode through the night and the next day, stopping only long enough to let Old Pony rest briefly. His mind burned with his hatred for his uncle, and blind fury kept him in the saddle hour after long hour. He took no notice of the direction he traveled, only that if he stopped he would dissolve in tears, and warriors did not cry.

Finally, Old Pony's exhaustion pierced his grief when the horse stumbled and almost went down. They stopped. Two Feathers slid off.

"I am sorry." He stroked the horse's neck until its breathing became easier. "You have carried me well. Your thoughts are only on what I need, and my thoughts have not been of your needs. You are a better friend to me than I am to you." He leaned his head against Old Pony's shoulder. "You are now my only friend. I will do better."

Two Feathers and his horse stood together in companionable silence until they had rested enough to move on. Exhaustion numbed his mind, making him focus on staying upright instead of his trouble with Yellow Hawk. He led Old Pony and looked for a camping spot. After an hour, he topped a low swell in the prairie. Below, in a shallow draw, a creek wound its way through cottonwood and sycamore trees. The smell of water quickened Old Pony's pace.

About dusk, Two Feathers lay still in the grass. A rabbit hopped slowly down a faint trail toward the stream. He hoped his stomach would not growl and scare it away. The rabbit stopped at the snare hidden under dried leaves and twigs. It sniffed. It hopped over the loop. Caught! Two Feathers jumped up, grabbed the animal, and sighed with relief. At the end of the shallow draw, he built a small fire under a sycamore tree so the smoke would filter through the leaves and not be seen. Soon, his stomach did not feel so empty.

Spreading his sleeping skins on the ground, he picked up the bundle Weeping Woman had left him at the tepee door. He opened it and buried his face in the soft deerskin clothing. The familiar smoky smell reminded him of her. When his parents would bring him to the village so his mother could visit her, Weeping Woman always had a gift for him. One time it was a wooden whistle, and another time it was a small horse she had made from the clay along the creek and baked in the coals. Wondering what she was doing now, he ran his hand over the deerskin shirt and pants she had made for him. *Weeping Woman, did I do right to leave? Yellow Hawk is my enemy. I could not stay. I have no grandfather or uncle to guide me. Who will show me the way?*

Two Feathers went to the creek and splashed his face. He sat on the bank and watched a large sycamore leaf drift by on the current. A cool breeze fanned the heat from his face, and the words of Weeping Woman floated across his mind.

"Always remember the teachings of your father and the ways of your mother."

How many times had Weeping Woman whispered those words in his ear so Yellow Hawk would not hear? He had a father to guide him and a mother to teach him the ways of his people. All he had to do was remember.

Two Feathers looked again at the bundle. He picked up the moccasins wrapped in his new shirt, then examined the ones on his feet. *No, not yet. The old ones will last a while longer.* Tucked in each moccasin, he found a package wrapped in deerskin and tied with narrow strings of hide. When he opened them, several small pouches filled with herbs spilled into his lap. They had spent many hours collecting in the fields and woods near their village. He wished now he had paid more attention when she told him their uses.

Two larger pouches held jerked meat and pemmican. Weeping Woman knew how much he liked the mixture of dried meat, fat, and berries. She knew it could save his life in an emergency. He remembered the musky smell of her as she comforted him when he grieved for his mother. He remembered the days she had spent teaching him the lessons of the prairie and the forest. Those lessons had kept him away from Yellow Hawk when the rage over the death of his only sister would fill him and spill over the small boy.

Why did the soldiers come that day? How did they know where we camped? The memories of the day of death filtered through the mental barriers he had set. *My father would not tell them. He would not betray my mother or her people.* Grief settled in the pit of his stomach like a stone. *No! Yellow Hawk hated my father because he was white and because he took my mother away. He hates me because I am my father's son.*

His mind settled once again about his father's innocence, Two Feathers looked toward the creek in time to see the sycamore leaf tumble over the ripples and disappear around a bend. He remembered coming from their cabin to visit and hearing the stories Weeping Woman told of his mother growing up in the village. He remembered the stories of his mother and Weeping Woman laughing by the creek, of splashing each other as they filled their water pouches. With these memories fresh in his mind, he stretched out on his sleeping skins. Knowing Old Pony would alert him of any danger, he slept.

On the third day, with the sun barely peeking over the horizon, Two Feathers rolled everything in the sleeping skins. Tying the bundle with leather strips, he slung it across his back with his bow and quiver and walked to the patch of grass where he had staked his pony. It nickered softly as Two Feathers walked up. He took the horse to the creek, and Old Pony drank deeply.

Two Feathers knew he had been in this camp long enough and needed to move. Old-man-with-gray-hair-on-his-face would see his tracks coming to and from the campsite if he stayed too long in one place. He had seen the man riding out in front of the herd, scouting the trail. Something about that man seemed familiar, but he could not remember why. He worked to stay away from the old man on the brown horse.

"You are my good friend," Two Feathers said to Old Pony as he rubbed the horse's head and scratched behind his ears. "You are a gift from my father. Many seasons have passed since the day the soldiers came, but as long as I have you, I have my father." Grabbing a handful of mane, he nimbly swung up on Old Pony. Settling on the saddle pad, he smoothed out a tangle in the long hair. "I know you are tired. We will catch the dunnia, and you can spend your days filling your belly on prairie grass. With your help, I will have a warrior's horse and will not need to follow a chief like Yellow Hawk. I will be the chief warriors will follow."

Two Feathers rode all day to get ahead of the herd, being careful to stay out of sight of old-man-with-gray-hair-on-his-face. Near a series of rolling hills, he tied the pony where it could graze. He worked his way to an outcropping of rocks. Hidden there, Two Feathers watched the herd without being seen. The boy on the dunnia and an older man on a bay horse worked at the head of the long line of cattle. A steer broke away, and the dunnia took after it. With the animal's quick start and sharp turns, Two Feathers knew the boy would fall off. But he stayed on the yellow horse and pushed the steer back in with the herd.

The remuda moved between his hiding place and the cattle. The gray horse stopped to grab a quick bite of grass. His head lifted. Long grass hung from his mouth. He looked straight at the rocks where Two Feathers hid. The Indian blinked, shook his head, and frowned, knowing the horse could not catch his scent because he was downwind. *It is too far for him to see me.* He puzzled at the animal's behavior. The gray moved away from the rest of the horses and toward the rocks. He stopped, lifted his head, and sniffed the wind. *This horse knows the prairie. He has not always been with whites.* The horse turned and trotted after the rest of the remuda.

As the long afternoon passed, the sun warmed the rocks where Two Feathers hid, and his water pouch slowly emptied. He had decided to find a shady campsite when he noticed a small calf that had somehow lost its mother and lagged behind the herd. The dunnia started to go after it, but the man called out. The white boy, who through the course of the day had moved to the end of the herd, repeatedly pointed to the calf, but the man motioned for him to come and rode off. The dunnia didn't follow. When the man's angry words cracked the air, the boy took a quick glance at the calf and rode toward camp.

Two Feathers settled again among the hot rocks, forming a plan. He watched the calf. The animal would start. Stop. Look around. Walk a little way. Bawl. Soon a good distance stretched between it and the herd. The calf walked to the shade of a bush and lay down. Two Feathers looked for its mother, but she was nowhere around. If she did not find her calf, his plan would work.

Slipping back through the rocks to his pony, behind the cover of the low hills, he moved away from the herd. A grove of oak trees provided enough cover for a camp. He staked his pony on some grass not too far away. The last of his dried meat, with some rather shriveled wild onions he had found earlier in the day, made his evening meal. He spread his sleeping skins on the ground and stretched out.

Two Feathers thought about the calf sleeping under the bush and hoped the boy and not its mother would find it. With the Great Spirit's help, tomorrow he'd have not only meat but the dunnia.

He waited for the night.

THE CALF

Will lay awake long into the night, planning how to rescue the calf that strayed behind the herd. Pa had told him its mother would find it. But he didn't think so. The herd had moved too far away. A plan settled in his mind. Finally, with his hand on the green ribbon, he drifted to sleep.

The next morning, Will stayed in his blankets and went over his plan till Pa had gone with Mr. Goodnight and most of the men had finished breakfast. He rolled his bedroll and tossed it in the chuck wagon. Plate in hand, he walked over to Cookie at the fire.

"About time you showed up," barked Cookie. "Ain't much left, but eat up what's there."

"Cookie," Will said between bites, "where you gonna make noon camp?"

"Smokey says there's a grove of oak trees about five miles due south. I've enough water in the barrels to make it to night camp, so we'll noon there."

Will walked over to where Hank and Curtis stood finishing their breakfast. Hank's mustache twitched as he smiled. Will couldn't help but laugh when he watched Hank eat. His long, bushy mustache wiggled up and down as he chewed, like a hairy caterpillar inching across his lip.

"Where ya ridin' today, Will? I'm at swing on this side," said Hank.

"I dunno. Maybe flank or maybe drag." He looked down at his plate and avoided the older man's eyes.

"I'd think you'd had enough of drag yesterday," Curtis said.

"Don't you be ridin' drag just to get an extra treat at the end of the day." Cookie took Will's empty plate and dumped it in the wash bucket. "It ain't fair to expect special treatment every night."

"I won't," Will said and ran for the remuda. He didn't want Cookie asking him any questions about where he was going to ride.

Buck came up as soon as Will reached the corral, and Naldo let him out through the rope gate. Will climbed on a large rock and smoothed the saddle blanket. He reached for the heavy saddle, but Curtis placed it on Buck and tightened the cinch. Much to Will's disgust, he grabbed him and tossed him in the saddle, nearly knocking his new hat off.

"You gonna ride drag again, Will-boy?"

Will settled himself in the saddle. "I dunno where I'll ride. Maybe swing on the far side of the herd."

"Well, I won't be seein' you till supper then." He grinned. "I'm ridin' flank on this side. Be careful out there."

"I'll be careful."

Relieved Curtis hadn't invited him to ride flank, he rode toward the herd and met Pa.

"I was looking for you," Pa said. "Smokey went to Fort Chadbourne to get information about any Comanche in the area. He saw a few unshod horse tracks. Charlie told me to scout ahead for water, a camping spot for tonight, and the best grazing. I'll be gone most of the day. You stay close to the herd." Pa started to ride off, then turned in the saddle and hollered back, "And check in with Cookie."

"Okay," Will called without looking at his father. He sat frozen in the saddle. Fear roared in his ears so loud all other sound faded. *Comanche! I didn't plan on Comanche.*

Pa spurred his horse and rode away. Will held Buck so he wouldn't follow. *How can I find that calf with Comanche around?* Buck shifted his weight in impatience. Will held him still. *Maybe its ma found it, and I won't have to go.* He gripped the saddle horn till his hand ached. Leaning forward, he hunched his shoulders, and his head dropped. Air whistled through his nose as he sucked in a deep breath. *Well, it has to be done. I don't care if Pa thinks it's okay for a ma and her kid to be separated. I know that calf needs its ma. I'll keep a sharp lookout.* Will blew out the air, kicked Buck into a lope, and rode to the herd. His heart pounded. He wiped his sweaty palms on his pants.

The drovers whooped, hollered, and popped their lariats. Almost as one, the cattle lunged to their feet. Ol' Blue took his place in the lead. The herd followed the clang of the big steer's bell south toward the Colorado River.

As Will worked through the morning, he looked for that calf and its mother but didn't see them. By noon, he'd made sure he'd worked every position except drag and spoken to each drover. The last thing he wanted was for someone to come looking for him.

At noon camp, he picked at his food and took his time finishing his lunch. *Dang it, Cookie. Hurry. I need all afternoon to find that calf and bring it back,* he thought. *If Pa gets back before I do, the jig is up.* Frustrated, he chewed his lip until it puffed red. He hung around camp, waiting for Cookie to pack and move to the night camp. To hurry things along, he helped as the old man hobbled around camp, packing the chuck wagon and hooking up the team. Will handed the last box up to Cookie. The old cook settled himself stiffly on the wagon seat. *Finally.* Will sighed in relief.

"I'm gonna work on the other side of the herd this afternoon," he said.

Cookie didn't pay much attention, just nodded and slapped the reins on the rumps of the team. Will had counted on this and lit a shuck for Buck.

The sun beat down hot and dry. Will pulled his bandana over his nose against the thick dust as he worked with Rory at drag. The drovers spread out, allowing the herd to widen. The dust settled a bit. He spotted the mother of that calf as she broke away from the herd and tried to head back toward last night's camp. Rory spun his horse after her and drove her back.

"That durn cow has lost her calf. She keeps trying to go back after it," Rory told Will.

"Why can't you let her go back?"

"We'd never get these critters to New Mexico if we let every cow that lost her calf go back to get it. She'll forget in another day or so," he said as his horse took off after her again.

I knew I'd have to get that calf. She may forget him, but I bet he'll not forget her.

Will slipped farther and farther behind Rory and the herd. When the billowing dust hid the drovers and the cattle, Will turned Buck and kicked him into a lope. "Come on, Buck. Let's get this done and get back."

They headed back to the ground they had covered yesterday. His nerves on edge, he watched the brush close by the trail and searched the distant prairie for any movement. "Keep your eyes peeled, Buck. I don't want to run into any Comanche."

Will passed the spot where they'd camped the night before. He rode till he found the place where he had last seen the calf. Too many tracks from the herd made him search the ground farther out. His eyes didn't want to stay on the ground. They kept looking up for fear a Comanche would sneak up on him.

"Buck, if we see any sign of unshod horses, we're getting out of here, calf or no calf."

Sweat turned Will's shirt and Buck's coat dark. They came to a shallow draw that moved away from the trail and turned down it. He spotted a small hoofprint and smiled.

"Look, Buck. We've got him now."

They rounded a boulder, and there he stood—next to a pool in the bend of a stream. Will patted Buck's neck. "I don't know which is prettier, that calf or that water." He took his lariat from his saddle, swung out a loop that landed over the little fellow's head, and wrapped the end around the saddle horn.

Will took a good look around for any sign of Indians. The thought of the long, hot ride back to the herd made him sweat even more. The cool water seemed to call his name. After another long, searching look for Comanche, temptation got the better of him, and he slid out of the saddle and tied the calf to a stout tree.

"Don't you worry. Buck and me will get you back to your ma." He threw his hat on the ground next to a low bush, pulled off his clothes, and jumped into the pool. He threw water at Buck as the horse bent his head and took a big drink. "Get a quick drink. You're supposed to be watching. We ain't stayin' here long. I don't want a Comanche sneaking up on us, especially in my long johns."

Will climbed out of the pool and reached for his hat. Death rattled under it.

He jerked his hand away and tumbled backward. Buck reared high, smashing his hooves down on Will's new hat. Again, he reared. Again, he smashed. The hat lay crumpled and torn. The rattle stopped. Buck backed away, trembling. He pawed the ground and shook his head. Will carefully lifted what was left of his hat. The bloody rattlesnake lay motionless.

"Buck." He grabbed the horse around the neck and hugged him tight. "That snake could have killed me."

He leaned his head against his best friend until his heart slowed its wild beating. He breathed easier. Picking up his clothes, he carried them to the shade near the calf and pulled them on. His new hat lay in a crumpled heap that barely resembled what he had put on his head that morning. He did his best to wash the blood off in the creek. He whacked it against his leg a few times, then poked, pushed, and twisted until it came close to a cowboy hat. Turning the brim in his hands, he sighed, then settled the mess on his head.

Suddenly, his stomach rolled over. It threatened to roll right out his mouth. He rushed back to Buck, grabbed the bridle, and pulled the long head down to look into his eyes. "What am I going to tell Pa? He's gonna be mad when he sees my hat."

Buck shook his head and rattled the bit in his mouth.

Will paced back and forth. "If I tell him about the snake, he'll make me ride next to him for days. That's the last place I want to be." He paced a few more laps. "Well . . . I can't help it. I can't hide my hat. So . . . I guess I just won't think about that snake right now." He looked at Buck. "If Ma were here, she would fix it with Pa. She was good at that."

The sparkle of the sun on the water caught his attention. "I'll bet there's fish in there. Maybe catfish. Pa loves catfish. That might fix things with him." He pulled out the string and a hook he always carried in his saddlebag. "You watch for Comanche. I'll catch some fish for Pa."

He looked around for a likely place to find worms. A decaying tree lay on the other side of the creek at the edge of some willows. Will found a narrow place to cross with enough rocks to make stepping stones. He picked up a stick and dug in the rich dirt under the hollow log. He soon found several large worms.

A short way up the creek, he found a spot where the bank hung over the water. He grinned. *I'll bet this is a good hidey-hole for fat fish.* He sat on the ground and tossed his hook in. It landed below the undercut bank. Before his worm had time to sink low in the water, it was gone. He jerked his line, and a bluegill sunfish landed on the bank.

"Buck, look at this one!" He held the flopping fish high in the air.

Buck lifted his head from his grassy snack. He looked at Will's fish and snorted.

"It may not look good to you," Will laughed, "but I can't wait for a crispy mouthful." A fresh worm went on his hook. He took off his battered hat, and the hot breeze dried his wet hair. His supply of worms dwindled, but the willow branch stringer soon filled with sunfish and even a fat catfish.

Will dozed in the cool shade of the willows as his stringer of fish bobbed in the creek, tied to a low-hanging branch. The buzz of a bee startled him and, when he looked up, he was alarmed to find that the sun had moved lower in the sky. He got up and hurriedly brushed the dirt and leaves off the seat of his pants. Once more he put on the crumpled hat and crossed the stepping stones back to the calf tied to the tree.

"Come on, Buck," he hollered. "We'd better head back to the herd. If Pa gets there before we do, he'll be plenty mad."

Buck came to him, and Will climbed onto a log to reach the saddle. He put his string and hook back in one saddlebag and the fish in the other.

Whack! Something hit him hard on the back. His face smacked the ground. With a startled cry, Will looked up.

A lanky Indian leaped over him and into the saddle. He kicked Buck, and the startled horse leaped into a gallop. Water splashed high as they crossed the creek. The Indian held tight to the mane, his legs gripping the sides of the saddle, stirrups flapping wildly.

Buck lowered his head, kicked out his back feet, and jumped straight up. He landed on stiff legs. The rider slipped in the saddle. Running hard, Buck headed back across the creek. The frightened calf bawled and ran to the end of his rope. Buck ran under a low-hanging limb. The Indian hit the ground hard. He didn't move.

Buck returned to Will, who was sprawled on the ground. The horse nudged Will's shoulder. He sat up. Blood dripped from his nose and cut lip. He spotted the Indian lying on the ground near the calf. With his heart threatening to burst through his ribs, Will scrambled onto the log and jumped into the saddle. Ignoring his bloody, aching nose, he grabbed the reins and went around the back of the tree, away from the Indian, to the frightened calf.

"Come on, calf. Let's get out of here." Will leaned down and pulled his rope loose, wrapping the end around the saddle horn, and the three of them headed back up the draw as fast as that little calf could move.

Will looked back over his shoulder at the Indian sprawled motionless on the ground. The feathers in his hair fluttered in the wind. Will gasped. His pounding heart kicked up a notch. "Buck, the cemetery! Remember? That's the same Comanche."

TROUBLE

Two Feathers sat up in time to watch the boy ride off on the dunnia. He dropped his head into his hands and winced as he explored the throbbing lump on his forehead. Blood covered his fingers and trickled down his face. He gasped at the sight of it and staggered to his feet. His throat stung, and his dry mouth made his tongue feel thick. At the creek, he dunked his head in the cool water and drank. For a long time, he sat on the bank with his pounding head in his hands. Failure stuck him to the ground. Failure sickened his stomach. Failure stole his confidence.

When he finally stood, it took a few minutes before he felt steady enough to move. The ground in front of him wavered. He stumbled to where he had fallen. He kicked the thick broken limb on the ground. *The yellow horse knocked me off.* His heart felt like a cold lump in his chest. He dropped to the ground, held his knees tight to his chest, and buried his face in the crook of his arm. *Not even the trees should see my shame.* He sat until his muscles screamed for release, and he eased the tight grip on his knees. When he looked up, his shadow stretched long in front of him. *It is good that Barks Like Coyote did not see me fall. Or Yellow Hawk.*

He splashed his face again. The water helped him feel better. The mud where Two Feathers lay on the bank cooled his skin against the heat of the day. *Weeping Woman, what do you make for Yellow Hawk when he comes home wounded from battle? What eases his fever and pain? My head hurts. What is the tea?*

Two Feathers sat up and spotted the long, drooping branches of a tree across the creek. A willow. He remembered. After cutting strips of bark with his knife, he made his way to Old Pony, tucked the bark in a pouch that hung from the saddle, and mounted. His head pounded with every step the horse made. He closed his eyes to the pain. Soon, his head drooped. The pony plodded on.

The clouds made a thin, orange line on the horizon. Only the tip of the hot, red sun remained when Two Feathers awoke. He looked around. Old Pony had brought him safely back to camp. He slipped off and staggered as his feet touched the ground. He hobbled the horse so it could graze and reach water but not get too far away. Taking out a cup he had found at an old campsite, he dipped from the creek and drank.

A fallen limb from the big cottonwood shading his camp provided twigs and sticks, and Two Feathers soon had a small fire burning. He balanced the cup of water on a rock at the edge of the fire. When the water was hot, he dropped in pieces of the willow bark. The tea tasted bitter, but he made himself drink the whole cup.

The coals blurred a fuzzy orange and red. They pulsed to the pounding in his head as he sat by the fire and stared. He blinked, and his vision cleared. *Maybe I should go back to the village. Weeping Woman would heal my head.*

A small animal scurried through the underbrush. Two Feathers rested his aching head on his knees. Loneliness hung on him like the weight of a buffalo robe. He sniffed and rubbed his eyes. *I will not go back to Yellow Hawk. I will follow the dunnia. The warrior's horse will be mine.* Wrapped in his sleeping skins, he turned his back to the fire and slept.

At first light, Two Feathers brewed another cup of the willow tea. The throbbing in his head felt somewhat better, but his stomach growled. After eating the last of his dried meat, he collected his things, packed them on his pony, and removed the hobbles.

The boy knows of me. The white men who drive the cattle will send old-man-with-gray-hair-on-his-face to hunt me. I will make a new camp where the whites cannot find me, and I will hunt. Fresh meat will make me strong again. Then I will take the dunnia.

Once mounted, he rode into the creek to hide his tracks. Coming to a gravel bar, he dismounted and waded back to the place where they had entered the water. Using dead leaves and twigs, he covered Old Pony's hoofprints. Two Feathers hoped that, by hiding their tracks, he would slow down old-man-with-gray-hair-on-his-face enough to get away.

The morning light warmed him as they waded up the creek bed. Old Pony's hooves splashed water into the air. It sparkled in the sunlight. The plaintive *coo-coo-coo* of a mourning dove lifted his spirits, and the loneliness of the night before faded. He came to a rocky ledge leading up out of the water. Knowing he would leave no tracks, they walked out on the flat rocks. He looked up at the sun, then headed south through the scattered trees and rolling hills.

Old Pony plodded on through the long, hot morning. Two Feathers's head began to pound again. He squinted into the sun beating straight down. The bump on his forehead was tender and burned when sweat rolled into it. All morning he watched his back trail, but no one followed. He needed to find a shady stream and brew more of the willow tea.

Two Feathers stopped just past the top of a hill. Below, he spotted a narrow band of green trees and grass. Old Pony perked up his ears and sniffed the air.

"You smell water? I hope you are right." They headed that way.

At the creek, he spied lots of animal tracks in the mud. "Rabbit tracks and good grass. We will eat well tonight, my old friend."

Two Feathers removed his packs and saddle. Old Pony tucked his knees under him, lay down, and rolled in the grass and leaves on the ground. He scrambled to his feet and shook the debris from his coat. Two Feathers brushed him with handfuls of dried grass until his old coat shone.

With camp made under the spreading limbs of an old live oak, Two Feathers heated his cup of water over a small fire and dropped in some willow bark. While it steeped, he set two snares near the stream.

Taking his cup, he moved up the hill and into the shadows of the trees. Two Feathers stood, sipping the bitter tea, and watched his back trail. The song of the cicadas and the tearing of grass as his pony grazed were the only sounds. His presence stilled the birds and squirrels. His eyes swept slowly over the low rolling hills and shallow valleys, looking for any movement. A faint dust cloud rose a long way back down the trail. He gasped, and hot tea spilled over his hand as he moved away from the tree. He shaded his eyes from the bright afternoon sun and studied the dust that hung in the air. It came straight up his trail.

Old-man-with-gray-hair-on-his-face comes.

Two Feathers hurried to move his camp. He grabbed up the snares and pulled clumps of grass to brush out their tracks.

After following the creek for about an hour, he came to a spot with thick indigo bushes growing between the tree trunks. He found a deer trail leading into a small clearing in the brush. The grass inside was flattened. When he spied deer droppings, Two Feathers grinned. *A doe has bedded her fawn here. I will be safe.* The trees spread a thick canopy over the opening so the smoke from his fire would spread out and not be seen. He walked out of the thicket and looked back to see how well his camp was hidden. Only his footprints showed. He took a handful of leafy branches and wiped them out.

Two Feathers took Old Pony to a grassy area near the stream and hobbled him. "Eat your fill, my friend. Then I will bring you into the thicket." He looked around. "Old-man-with-gray-hair-on-his-face will not find us here."

The rumble from his stomach reminded him he had eaten the last of his meat early that morning. He took his bow and quiver and followed the stream about a mile upwind from his camp. He spotted a doe eating seedpods that hung from the limbs of a mesquite tree. Two Feathers nocked his arrow in the bowstring, pulled it back as far as it would go, and let it fly. The deer stumbled, ran a few yards, and fell. Two Feathers ran to the deer and pulled out his arrow. *Barks Like Coyote could not make such a good shot,* he thought. He licked his lips, picturing all the dried meat it would make and the fresh liver he would eat. Two Feathers skinned it quickly and cut the meat into hunks. He wrapped them in the skin and carried the bundle to camp.

On the way back, he spotted a dead tree covered with grape vines loaded with summer fruit. The sight of plump purple grapes made his mouth water. He grabbed a few as he went by. *I will eat well tonight.* At camp, he hung his meat bundle from a limb to keep it out of reach of hungry predators, and then he broke a large curved section of bark from the trunk of a fallen tree.

Two Feathers took his makeshift basket and went back to the tree where he had killed the deer. The doe had eaten many of the low-hanging mesquite pods, so Two Feathers climbed onto the lower branches to reach those growing higher up. His growling stomach helped him ignore the scrapes and pricks from the mesquite thorns. At the fallen tree, birds and animals had found the grapes before Two Feathers. But even with the ones he popped into his mouth, he picked enough so that, with the bean pods, he carried a full basket back to camp.

Two Feathers sat and rested his head against a tree, watching the red, orange, and purple shift and fade in the western sky. A hunk of deer liver sizzled over the fire on a green stick, braced on a notched branch stuck in the ground. He looked around and knew he had made a good camp. The savory aroma of cooking meat teased his nose and made his hunger rumble. The day had been long. He had worked hard. Weeping Woman would be pleased.

More branches held strips of meat that hung drying near the fire. Stakes driven into the ground held the deerskin he had scraped clean of meat and fat with the dull side of his knife. The brains of the deer he had worked into the hide would cure it. Soon it would make pouches to carry food and moccasins for his feet.

He lifted the hot liver, still running red, from over the fire. It burned his fingers and mouth but filled his stomach. The fresh liver, his favorite, moved him from full to stuffed. A feeling he had not had in a long time. Two Feathers chewed the sweet mesquite pods and grapes. They made the bitter willow tea easier to swallow. The tea eased the dull ache in his head. He knew he should go to the hill before dark and look for old-man-with-gray-hair-on-his-face, but he was tired and full and his camp well hidden. He finished the tea, rolled in his sleeping skins, and turned his back to the glow of the coals.

FEAR

Will heard a rustle in the brush. He turned his head to see his mother standing under a tree. She pointed behind him. He turned. A Comanche leaped at him from the brush with a knife raised. Will screamed. No sound came. The Indian crept closer and closer. The knife rose higher and higher. Something grabbed him from behind and shook him.

"Will, wake up." Pa shook his shoulder.

Will's eyes opened. "He's after me. That Comanche is after me."

"There's no Indian here, son. You had a nightmare. Sit up a minute and take a deep breath."

Will looked around at the sleeping men in their blankets and the glowing coals of the campfire.

"You're okay. Try to go back to sleep."

Lying back down, he pulled his blankets over his head, his heart still banging. His hand slipped in his pocket and rubbed the green ribbon till he fell asleep.

The next morning, he woke to find the men already lined up to fill their plates.

"Hey, sleepyhead. You gonna stay in your blankets all day?" Jake teased.

Will reached for his boots and shook them out. A scorpion hit the ground. He scrambled out of its way, then crushed it under his boot heel.

"Hey, Tony. Did you see that scorpion? It was a big one." He pulled his boots on and rolled his blankets. Then he picked up his smashed new hat, turned it over and over, frowned, and tossed it into the chuck wagon with his bedroll.

One of the twins handed Will a plate. "Load up before we eat it all."

Will grinned at the two look-alikes. "Thanks, Tony."

"I'm Jake. That's Tony stuffin' his ugly face."

Pa walked up with his plate. "You think by the end of the drive we'll be able to tell which is Jake and which—"

"No." Will cut him off, still mad from the scolding he'd gotten last night when he brought the calf back to the herd. "Hey, you two. Wait, and I'll go with you." He dumped his plate in the wash bucket and took off after the twins.

"Whoa." Pa caught Will by the arm. "You're not going any-where today. Remember? You have three days to ride with Cookie."

"That's not fair." A rush of anger made his face burn. "I told you I had to get that calf. He needed his ma."

"I know, but I told you to stay with the herd. A good cow-boy doesn't disobey his boss. I can't have that. Not only have you ruined an expensive hat, you risked your life for a calf that might not survive the drive. Smokey had to leave his scouting responsibilities to look for that Indian. I said to ride the chuck wagon for three days, and that's what you'll do."

Pa walked to the remuda, saddled the horse Naldo had roped for him, mounted, and rode toward the herd. He didn't look back at Will.

Will watched Pa ride away. He turned to the fire and kicked dirt into the flames. "Calves are supposed to have a ma," Will mumbled.

"If we're going to be partners for three days, I'd appreciate it if you didn't kick dirt into my last cup of coffee." Cookie picked up the pot from the fire and poured a cup.

Will looked up at him. "Sorry, but I don't see why he's making me stay here. I can look after myself."

Cookie took a sip of coffee. "That may be true, but it doesn't change the fact that you and I are partners for the day, so let's make the best of it. What do you say?"

Will sighed loudly and frowned at Cookie. "What do I have to do?"

"Empty the coffee pot over the fire. Spread the coals so they'll burn out. Go get the team from Naldo, and help me hitch the wagon. We need to get moving if we're going to find a lunch site and get the grub ready by noon." While Cookie packed the rest of the gear into the chuck wagon, Will ran to Naldo for the mules.

Buck met him at the corral, and Naldo let him out. Will scratched under the long mane. "You have a three-day vacation while I ride in the wagon and fetch and carry for old Cookie," he said as Buck nudged him. "You stay with the remuda. I've got enough trouble without worryin' about you. Naldo, I'm supposed to bring the wagon team."

Two mules stood tied to a tree. "Take these grays. You sure you can handle them? I can call one of the boys to help you."

"No thanks." He took the lead ropes and started back toward camp, dragging the team behind him. "I can handle 'em. Come on, mules. We don't have all day." The big animals tossed their heads and kicked up puffs of dust as they plodded along.

Cookie grinned at Will's sweating face as the slow-moving team came into camp and stopped at the wagon. "Fritz goes on the right and Ben on the left."

"I don't know which is which." Will pulled his bandana from around his neck and wiped his face. "Naldo just said to bring these grays."

"Fritz is the darker one. Put him on the right. Mules are a lot like people. They get in the habit of a certain spot, and they don't like to change."

Cookie lifted the harness onto Fritz's back, straightened the lines, and secured the crupper under the mule's tail. He took the heavy collar from Will, lifted it to the mule's neck, and settled it on the broad shoulders. Cookie worked with sure hands and quickly fastened the buckles and straps, then slipped the bridles over each mule's head. Fritz took his bit without complaint, but Ben twisted and jerked his head.

"Whoa, Ben. What's got into you? Your mouth still a bit tender?"

"What's wrong with his mouth?" Will looked up as the mule rattled the bit in his teeth and worked his tongue around it.

"He had a sore spot the other day. I told Naldo to let him rest a while. He should be all right by now. Hook up the reins, and be sure you don't get them backward."

"I know how to hitch a team." He flipped the reins over Fritz's back and clipped the short end to the outside of his bit and the long side to the inside of Ben's bit. Then he did the same with Ben's reins.

"Back, Fritz. Back, Ben." Gnarled hands pulled on the reins, and the mules backed up. Cookie hooked the team to the doubletrees on the wagon, and they were set to go.

Will stepped up on the wheel hub and into the wagon. His old hat lay on the seat. He looked at it, frowned, and then jerked it down tight. Cookie pulled himself up on the wagon seat.

"I see you found your hat."

"My old hat." Will shuddered when he thought of the rattlesnake.

Cookie flicked the reins. They headed south toward the Colorado River.

The morning seemed to last forever as Will heard story after story of Cookie's bronc-busting days. His bottom hurt from bouncing and bumping on the wagon seat. With each new story, the horses became wilder and kicked harder. Cookie was thrown farther and higher. The number of horses he tamed grew and grew.

At the noon camp, Will gathered firewood, carried water, poured coffee, and worked hard to be sure he avoided Pa. Whenever the cowboys teased him about doing camp chores, he grinned and reminded them of how good all that fried fish tasted, and if they wanted more, they better watch out.

The afternoon was a repeat of the long, boring morning. *It's not fair* echoed through Will's mind as he bounced on the wagon seat, ignoring Cookie's chatter. Pa hadn't listened when he tried to explain that the calf he went after belonged to one of their cows. *How am I supposed to be a cowboy if I can't do the work?*

Day two was the same as day one. Will watched all afternoon for Smokey, but the old scout didn't return.

"When's Smokey getting back? Do you think he found that Comanche?" Will stood in the wagon seat, grabbed the canvas cover, and leaned around to look back the way they had come.

Cookie grabbed Will's belt and pulled him back down. "Sit down before you fall out. You can ask Smokey all the questions you want when he gets here. I don't have any answers."

The wagon bumped over a rock. Will grabbed the seat before he bounced out. "What if that Indian gets Smokey? He was real mean. What if there's a whole war party of them?"

"Smokey can take care of himself. You don't need to worry about him."

That night, the drovers took turns coming into camp to eat supper. Will had about given up on Smokey when he saw him riding up with Pa and Mr. Goodnight. Cookie filled their plates. Smokey ate and told them what he'd found.

"I tracked Will and Buck to where they turned down the draw. The Indian picked up his trail there. He followed Will to the creek and crossed farther down. He must have jumped on Buck where he pushed Will off the log. Buck ran him under a branch and, from the size of it, he probably has a lump as big as a goose egg."

"I hope his head falls off," Will mumbled.

Cookie refilled Smokey's coffee cup.

"It looks like he lay at the creek for a time soaking his head. I got a good look at several footprints. They're of a boy about half grown. I found where he tied his horse. He's riding an old pony. Some gray hairs mixed with brown ones caught in the bark where it rubbed against a tree."

"See any sign of others around?" Mr. Goodnight asked.

"No. I tracked him a good way. He's alone. That's strange 'cause the Comanche don't usually let their young ride around by themselves. When they take their boys out, there's at least one man with them, usually more."

"Where is he? Did you capture him?" Will asked.

"No, I didn't. We have cattle to drive. We don't need an Indian boy complicating things. And if there are others looking for him, I didn't want to bring them here."

"Why would a lone Comanche boy be following the herd?" Goodnight said.

"He's no threat to the herd. It's not the cattle he's after," Smokey said. "For a Comanche, a fine horse would make him an important man in the village." He looked at Will. "He's after Buck."

That sick tobacco feeling hit Will hard, and his supper burned the back of his throat. Will dropped his plate and ran for the remuda.

Naldo had the horses grazing along a muddy creek near the camp. Will ran about halfway and stopped. Panic coursed through his veins like hot lava. He put his fingers to his lips and whistled.

Buck lifted his muzzle from the water and loped toward Will. Naldo let him go by and cut off the others that tried to follow. Buck trotted up to the boy and lowered his head. Will scratched behind his ears.

"You have to stay with me all the time now, Buck. That Comanche is trying to get you." Buck followed the boy as they walked back to camp.

"Pa, Buck is going to stay with me."

"Whoa, wait a minute," Mr. Goodnight said. "I understand you want to protect your horse. But, son, we can't have him living in the middle of camp. He'll have to stay with the remuda."

"Mr. Goodnight," said Will, "Buck's not a regular horse."

Charlie Goodnight pushed up his hat, scratched his head, and looked at Pa.

"Will," Pa said, "Naldo will take good care of him. He can't stay with you. He has to graze. He won't find enough to eat if he stays in camp. You know that."

"He has to stay with me. That Indian can't get him if he's in camp."

Goodnight and Smokey moved away from Dan and Will.

"He has to stay with the remuda, Will. Let's take him back. I'll tell Naldo to watch out for him."

Will didn't move. He narrowed his eyes and clenched his fists. "I'm not going to leave him like you left Ma."

Pa sucked in a deep breath then blew it out, jerked off his hat, and ran his hand through his hair. His face flushed red. He stared off across the herd for a long time. Then he said, "We are not on the ranch where you can sleep in the barn with him." He spoke with a tight voice. "It's dangerous out here. You have to stay in camp. Buck will be with the other horses, and Naldo will take good care of him." Pa picked up his lariat and slipped the loop around Buck's neck. "Come on, Will." His voice softened. "Remember when he was a colt, and you wanted to bring him in the house? This is the same thing. He can't stay in camp."

Will ducked his head and would not look at Pa. *I won't leave Buck,* he promised himself.

That night, Will lay on top of his blankets. Waiting. Listening. The air was still and hot. Pa lay nearby. When his deep breathing settled into a snore, Will sat up. He put a chunk of wood under his blanket and slipped away from camp. As quietly as he could, he headed for the remuda.

Will spotted Buck standing off to the side of the other horses. He called softly. The horse came to him. They walked to a cluster of trees and faded into the shadows.

"Buck," Will whispered, "we need to stay together. This is mean country. You don't need to be by yourself."

The boy curled up at the base of a tree and rested his head on his arm. Buck nudged the boy. Will looked up and rubbed the velvet nose. "I won't leave you. I promise."

Night creatures scurried through the darkness as an owl sailed by on silent wings. The big horse lifted his head. His ears flicked forward. His nostrils flared. He sniffed the wind, testing the scents blowing on the night breeze. Will settled himself on the hard ground and slept.

"Will," Naldo said as he dismounted near the big stallion. The moon worked its way out from behind a bank of clouds as he shook Will awake. "Amigo, you must go back to camp. Your papa will be angry if he finds you here."

Will sat up and rubbed his eyes. "No. I have to take care of Buck. That Indian can't get him."

"Don't worry. I'll take good care of him. Now go, before your papa finds you gone."

Will stood and planted himself under Buck's head, one arm lifted to the strong neck, fingers twisted in the long mane. "I'm not leaving. If he can't stay in camp, I'll stay with him."

"Your papa is not going to like you out here alone."

"I'm not alone. I'm with Buck."

THE COLORADO

Two Feathers remained in camp for several days. The fresh meat, grapes, onions, and mesquite pods helped him recover, and his head healed. Each day he worked the deerskin with water so it wouldn't dry too quickly and become stiff and hard. On the third day, he removed the hide from the pegs and rubbed it back and forth over a branch to make it supple.

The long afternoons passed quickly as he worked. When the camp in the thicket became too hot, he sat under the shade of a pecan tree near the creek. He cut long, narrow strings from the hide and sewed together several pouches. *They are not as nice as Weeping Woman's, but they will carry enough meat to keep my stomach quiet for a while.*

The sun rose a deep red from behind a bank of clouds on the morning Two Feathers decided he was ready to move on. Old Pony raised his muzzle and sniffed the wind. Two Feathers grinned. "You smell it, too? It won't be many suns till we have rain. It is time to get the dunnia."

He packed his food and loaded the bulging pouches behind the saddle. He slung his bow and quiver across his back and mounted. *Yellow Hawk could not live so long alone without Weeping Woman to cook his food and make his clothes. He wouldn't do women's work, but for the trail, it is good she taught me well. I have food to eat for many suns. I don't need to hunt every day or go hungry, as men on the trail do. She has helped me be a good warrior.*

Old Pony lifted his head, pulling on the reins, and stepped out.

"You ready to go?" Two Feathers laughed. "We will find the white man's cattle and make a plan. Soon we will have the dunnia."

By the time Two Feathers caught up with the herd, the white men were pushing them across a wide river. He hid in the grass and brush where he could see over the crest of a hill. As they came out of the water, they spread over the long grass waving in the wind. The remuda grazed on the opposite side of the campsite from the herd. He searched for the dunnia. The gray horse caught his attention. It moved away from the others, tested the air, and only then did it crop the grass. Even from a distance, Two Feathers could see the strength in the horse. *Where did you come from? What are you doing with the whites?*

Light danced and sparkled on the surface of the water. The grass and trees along the banks made a green ribbon as the river meandered through the brown and golden dried grama grass. A mourning dove called its plaintive *coo, coo, coo* from the willows that lined the riverbanks. A woodpecker pounded out its *rat-a-tat-tat*. The noon sun burned Two Feathers's back. He slid deeper under a mesquite bush and looked again for the yellow-horse-with-black-mane-and-tail. *There you are.* He grinned at the sight of the golden horse. The dunnia lifted his head. His mane and tail fluttered in the wind. He stood for a while. Two Feathers's heart beat with excitement. *Soon.*

A lone cloud drifted over the sun and brought a welcome, but short, relief from the heat. The white men took turns coming into camp to wash their clothes and blankets and draped them on bushes to dry. Two Feathers watched the boy splash one of the men as they washed their blankets. Suddenly, they peeled off their chaps and boots and jumped in the river. Faint laughter drifted to him on the breeze. Two Feathers rolled over on his back and watched the cloud float by.

John, kick your feet. You can do it. He heard his father's voice. *Swim to me. Kick hard. Just a little more.* He remembered the strong arms that had plucked him from the water. *See. I knew you could do it.* The sound of his father's laughter filled his ears. How proud he had been when he finally swam across the pond near their cabin, his mother watching and smiling from the porch.

John. My father's name, and my name, too. Two Feathers sat up. He smiled. He remembered. "John," he said aloud.

Two Feathers slipped down the back of the hill and rode his pony upstream. He wanted to be a good distance from the eyes of old-man-with-gray-hair-on-his-face. *Who is that old man? Why do I think of him when remembering my father?* Thoughts and memories swirled in his head as he rode.

Old Pony stopped and snorted. Two Feathers realized he had ridden a long time. The stream flowed through a small tree-lined gravel bar. An abundance of driftwood lay scattered about. He staked his pony in a small grove of pecan trees away from the creek and made camp.

For two suns, the cattle stayed by the river. Two Feathers watched the yellow horse and explored the country upriver, being careful not to leave tracks the old man could find. He found a new campsite farther from the cattle where the creek flowed through a small valley. *Tonight, I will bring the dunnia here.* Excited, he headed back toward the herd.

As night fell, Two Feathers and Old Pony watched from the cover of a cottonwood tree near where the creek flowed into the river. The remuda grazed between the cattle and the sparkling band of water. Some whites were coming in from the herd, and others were going out. The boy rode the dunnia in and turned him loose to graze. The tall chief of the whites saddled the gray horse and rode off.

Two Feathers stood there for a long time. Clouds began to gather, and the wind picked up. The moon rose and cast its dim light off and on through the drifting clouds. The-one-who-guards-the-horses moved the remuda farther away from the river. The flicker of the white men's campfire winked in the night. He listened to their distant voices. He stepped close to Old Pony and stroked his neck, then leaped astride. "Let's go get the dunnia."

Hoofbeats! He slid off and put his hand over the horse's muzzle to keep him quiet. A band of five Comanche rode out of the darkness, dismounted up the creek from where Two Feathers hid, and led their horses to drink. Two Feathers started to call, but when he heard Yellow Hawk's voice, he froze.

"We will cross the river there." Yellow Hawk pointed to where the creek flowed into the silver ribbon shimmering in the moonlight. "When we cross back, head the horses up the creek. We will run them all night."

They swung up on their mounts, and with a break in the cloud cover, Two Feathers recognized Running Wolf and Barks Like Coyote from his village. He watched as they walked their horses across the river. Then, at a run, they circled the remuda near the sleeping camp.

Anger filled him at the thought of Yellow Hawk taking the dunnia. He leaped astride Old Pony, and they galloped toward the river. Two Feathers heard the whoops and yells from the Comanche as they surrounded the horses. The angry shouts of the white men and the crack of their guns froze the blood in his veins and flashed memories of the screams of his people on the day of death.

Through the dark of the night, he heard the sound of pounding hooves and the splash of water as the Comanche drove the horses across the river and up the creek at a gallop. As they flashed past, he spotted the dunnia running in the middle of the bunch. He slumped with relief at the sight of the horse.

Yellow Hawk and Running Wolf ran at the head of the remuda. Barks Like Coyote and two others pushed them from the rear. Fury blinded Two Feathers to any thought but getting the dunnia away from his enemy. Old Pony burst into a gallop. Wind whipped the feathers in the boy's hair, and he bent low over the horse's neck. He yelled in the horse's ear and kicked him with his heels, driving him faster. But Yellow Hawk and the horses disappeared in the darkness. Old Pony stumbled. Two Feathers sat up straight and pulled on the reins, slowing the old horse. He reached down and patted the sweating neck.

"You would run until your heart burst if I asked you. I am sorry. I will not let my enemy make me harm you."

They followed the trail of the remuda at a lope. Plans to get the dunnia formed in his mind. He discarded each one as he remembered the skill of Yellow Hawk in capturing horses. *It will be hard to get the dunnia from my enemy. It is easy to get horses from the whites, but not from a Comanche.* Then he grinned. *I have seen the dunnia and the boy together. I know what will happen when he hears the whistle. Even Yellow Hawk cannot hold him. I will have him yet.*

Two Feathers and Old Pony followed Yellow Hawk through the moonless night. Lightning flashed. The clouds boiled and piled up into tall black mountains. A cool wind fanned Two Feathers's face. Yellow Hawk finally stopped and let the horses drink. When Two Feathers caught up, he called out and rode to his uncle.

Yellow Hawk scowled when he saw the boy dismount and walk toward him. "Where have you been? What are you doing here?"

"I have been hunting my horse." Two Feathers stood straight and looked his uncle in the eye, his heart drumming. "You have him. I will take him now."

Yellow Hawk snorted in disgust. "You? The dunnia is in the bunch I took. He is a warrior's horse, and you are not a warrior. You are a boy who likes woman's work."

Barks Like Coyote snickered. Two Feathers said nothing, but his anger flushed over him as he took his rope from Old Pony. He walked toward the horses and shook out a loop.

In three strides, Yellow Hawk barred his way. "You are not worthy of such a horse. You are not Comanche. You are white, like your father." He shoved Two Feathers to the ground and spat on him. "Go from here. You do not belong." Yellow Hawk turned his back on the boy and headed for his horse. "We will go," he said to the others. "A storm is coming."

With a shout of rage, Two Feathers leaped to his feet and jumped onto Yellow Hawk's back. He grabbed a handful of hair and jerked his uncle's head back. They fell to the ground. Yellow Hawk flipped the boy off and sprang to his feet. Leaping up, he drew his knife and pinned the boy to the ground with his foot. Two Feathers struggled against the big man's weight until he felt the knife against his throat.

Running Wolf caught Yellow Hawk's arm. "You will not kill this boy. He is your sister's child. Send him away. Keep the stallion, but send the boy away."

Yellow Hawk sheathed his knife, turned away, and mounted his horse. He rode toward the dunnia.

Running Wolf offered his hand to Two Feathers. He took it, and the older man pulled him to his feet.

"You must go. You have done well by yourself. You will be a strong warrior one day. But forget the dunnia. Now he is Yellow Hawk's horse."

Two Feathers stood still, his face hot with anger, his heart beating with deep hard thuds. He sucked in a long breath through his nose and exhaled sharply. He looked at Running Wolf. "You were a friend to my father. I will go, as you say, but the dunnia will not be my enemy's horse. I will have him."

Two Feathers mounted Old Pony and rode away from the creek. *The white boy's whistle will end Yellow Hawk's plans.* He spat on the ground.

THUNDERSTORM

Will's eyes flew open at the sound of shots. He stomped into his boots and grabbed his hat. "What's goin' on?" he asked as Pa pulled his rifle from the back of the chuck wagon.

"Comanche hit the remuda. They got about half the horses."

"Buck?" Will grabbed Pa's arm and jerked him to a stop.

"Yes, he's with 'em. Come on. Charlie wants you along."

"I knew that Indian would get him." His heart ricocheted in his chest. He yanked harder and spun Pa around. "This is your fault. You shoulda let Buck stay in camp."

Pa looked at Will and shook his head. "This is not the time to argue, Will. I'm sorry Buck is gone. We'll do the best we can to get him back."

Will stood, frozen. Fear tore at his stomach, its sharp sting crawling up the back of his throat. Will forced his legs to obey. He followed as Pa headed for the drovers gathered around the campfire. Will glared up at him and bit off any further accusations when they joined the men.

Cowboys moved with grim determination as they collected their gear and saddled horses. Shadows ebbed and flowed as thickening clouds sailed across the moon. The flickering light showed hard faces as the men gathered near the campfire.

"Russ, you and Hank go with us," Goodnight said. "Naldo, bunch the rest of the horses as close to the herd as you can. We don't want the Comanche doubling back and getting the rest. Mount up, boys. Smokey's already on the trail. Will, ride double with Dan. If Buck can break loose, he'll come to your whistle. Maybe the others will come with him."

The four men and Will headed across the Colorado and up the creek. The moon came from behind some clouds and bathed the riders with a silvery light. The men rode with hard faces. No one spoke. The horses' steady lope ate up the miles.

Will squirmed on his perch behind Pa's saddle. His legs began to ache from gripping the horse's flanks. He leaned from one side to the other, trying to see around Pa.

Pa patted Will's hands where they gripped his shirt. "Hang on. We should catch up with them soon."

Will let go of Pa's shirt and gripped the saddle.

Smokey rode up to them in a grove of oak trees. "They've turned due west. From the tracks, it looks like five of them. They're runnin' hard."

"Smokey, did you see Buck's tracks? Are you sure they got him?" Will leaned from behind Pa.

"They've got him."

"Comanche?"

Smokey nodded.

"That Indian got him. The one with the feathers. If he hurts Buck . . . " A cold knot filled Will's chest.

Smokey led out, following the tracks of the stolen horses. They rode for a couple of hours. Clouds began building, and lightning flashed in the distant sky. The darkness deepened. The air cooled, and the wind felt damp.

Smokey pulled up, and the others grouped around him. "They've slowed. I know this spot. The creek pools there and makes a good water hole."

"Scout ahead," Goodnight said. "We'll wait for you."

Smokey stepped off his horse and handed the reins to Goodnight. Digging a pair of moccasins from his saddlebag, he pulled off his boots and slipped them on instead, allowing him to move silently through the woods. "Give me a few minutes. Then come quiet. I'll find you, and we'll decide what to do." He slipped away in the darkness.

The men dismounted and stood in the cover of the trees. No one talked. No one moved. Each man held the reins of his horse. The clouds rolled and billowed in the sky. Lightning flashed briefly inside the clouds. Will blinked in the bright flash. He looked for the others in the darkness that followed, eyes blinded by the light. A horse shifted its weight and shook its head. Its bridle rattled in the stillness.

"Pa, how much longer?" Will whispered.

"Pretty soon."

A slight wind picked up. Will sucked in the sultry air. *How will we find Buck if it storms?* He turned again to Pa. A firm hand squeezed his shoulder. Will remained silent. *Buck, when we get back, you'll stay in camp.* He chewed his lip and searched the darkness for any sign of Smokey. *I'll make them let you. I promise.*

"Okay, boys. We've waited long enough. Let's go," Goodnight said, barely audible. The men mounted and walked their horses toward the distant creek. Not a man spoke.

Will tightened his hold on Pa. He looked for Smokey, but the darkness had swallowed him up. An occasional creak of a saddle or click of hooves on stones were the only sounds. As the trees that lined the stream drew nearer, a figure separated itself from the darker shadows and silently walked to the approaching men.

"We'd better hurry," whispered Smokey. "They stopped to water the horses, and now they're about to cross. I don't think this storm is going to hold off much longer." He pointed downstream and whispered instructions, then took his horse from Goodnight and mounted.

Goodnight, Russ, and Hank headed down the creek. Smokey, Will, and Pa waited a few minutes to give them time to get set.

"Will, when I tell you, whistle for Buck, and make it loud," Smokey said.

Will nodded.

The older man watched as the riders neared the creek. "Now."

Will put his fingers to his lips, and his whistle screamed through the darkness. Buck's answering call split the air.

"That's Buck!" Will shouted.

Wild yells erupted from downstream as the men headed across the creek. Pa and Smokey galloped into the trees as thunder boomed and rain flooded the sky. Will gripped tight to Pa's waist. Horses milled everywhere. Indians whooped and yelled. The drovers shot guns into the air, and the horses raced away from the creek. Lightning flashed.

Will spotted Buck. Two Indians had their ropes on him. He reared, hooves slashing the air.

"There he is," Will shouted as he leaned to look around Pa. "Look at him go!" He grabbed Pa's shoulders and pulled himself up enough to see, practically standing on the back of the saddle. "Get 'em, Buck. Ha, that'll teach 'em."

Buck jumped and kicked a horse out from under one Indian rider. Again he reared, his forefeet pawing the air. Teeth bared, his head shot forward, and he bit the other Indian's mount on the rump. The horse screamed and bolted, throwing its rider.

Shots rang out as Goodnight and Hank fired their rifles into the air, careful not to hit the horses.

The Comanche swung their fallen warriors up behind them and headed away from the creek, leaving the remuda behind. Their injured horses trailed after them.

Will watched them gallop away. One brave stopped on the crest of a hill. A flash of lightning showed yellow paint on one side of his face and black on the other. He raised his arm and shook his fist at the drovers. His voice boomed into the roaring rain and wind as he shouted in Comanche. He wheeled his horse and raced after the fleeing warriors.

Will tightened his grip on Pa's shirt and looked into the emptiness where his words had howled with the wind. "What did he say, Pa?"

"I don't know. But I sure don't like the way he said it."

The drovers collected the horses and headed them back toward the river through the downpour.

Buck shook himself, threw off the ropes, and blew hard. Will called. Buck trotted over, and Pa swung Will onto his back.

Will leaned over, wrapped his arms around the horse's neck, and hugged him tight. The big horse nickered softly. Will grabbed a handful of mane. "Go." They rode after Pa.

Will twisted his hands in the mane, and his knees squeezed Buck, but still he slipped on the horse's wet back. The raging storm dropped the temperature, and needles of cold water lashed his face and ran down his back. He pulled his wet hat tight over his eyes, but the driving rain blurred his vision.

In the harsh, blue light from a lightning flash, Will recognized the worried look on Pa's face as he turned his horse behind the remuda to push the stragglers ahead.

"Pa," Will shouted, "why are we drivin' 'em so hard? Buck's tired, and I don't want him slippin' in the mud."

"The river," Pa yelled back. "We have to cross before the runoff from upstream floods the river."

"Buck." The horse turned an ear back. "I don't swim so good. I sure hope you do."

Will wiped the streaming water from his face. His legs ached from gripping Buck, and the wet, cold wind made his hands stiff. Lightning flashed, silhouetting the dark figure of Pa ahead of him. Will rode after his father.

The tired horses began to lag, and the soaked drovers hollered, waving their hats and coiled lariats to keep them moving.

When they reached the river, Buck skidded to a stop. His eyes wide, he pranced in a circle and backed away from the edge.

"Oh, Buck. I don't like this." Will's heartbeat matched the racing river. The high water roiled and tumbled over boulders and bushes that had been high on the banks at their earlier crossing. Limbs and logs raced past.

"Will," Pa shouted. "We'll cross farther upstream. There's a gravel bar there."

Will turned Buck and followed. He chewed his lips as he watched the wild river. He pulled his hat as low as he could without blocking his sight. He watched Goodnight, on the grullo, ride into the river to lead the remuda. Russ and Hank pushed the horses off the gravel bar, and they swept downstream. Horses bobbed in the water as they swam for the bank on the opposite side. A log swept down on Curtis's Appaloosa, knocking him under. When he came up, he thrashed in the water in a panic, threatening to go under again. Hank turned his big sorrel alongside to steady him, and they swept out of sight.

"Will, ride upstream to the end of the gravel bar," Pa yelled. "Go in there. The current will carry you downstream. Head Buck for the bank where we crossed earlier. Hang on tight. If you get washed off, grab Buck's tail. He'll pull you out on the other side. I'll come in downstream, in case you get in trouble."

Will headed for the gravel bar. He watched a log smack into a rock and break in half before rushing on downstream. "I'm scared, Pa," Will yelled as the rain lashed him.

"So am I. Just hang on to Buck. He'll get you across. Go, Will. You have no choice."

Will watched as Pa jumped his horse into the river. He took a deep breath and kicked Buck's flanks. The big horse stepped into the current. Buck pranced, not liking the rush of water on his legs. He waded farther out. He stopped, eyes wide, then lunged off the gravel bar and into deep water. His powerful legs kicked as he swam into the swift current.

Water spilled over the tops of Will's boots, chilling his feet. He tried to call for Pa, but all he could do was gulp for air as the cold water gripped his stomach and took his breath. His hands twisted in Buck's mane as the rushing water lifted him off the horse. Kicking hard, he pushed his legs down and tried to get a grip on Buck, but the force of the water swept his legs over the horse's back.

Water filled Will's mouth and nose. Panicked, he coughed, sputtered, and sucked in air before the cold water washed over him again. His hands tangled in the mane, and he gripped with all his might. The force of the water swept him around to Buck's head. The big horse's hooves struck the rocky bottom, and he found his footing. Will kicked hard and pulled on the tangled mane. He gasped for air and swam onto Buck's back as the horse pulled himself out of the water and up the bank.

Will lay on his horse, clinging tight to the mane and sucking in great gulps of air. He couldn't tell if the roaring in his ears was the river or his fear.

Pa reached over to pull Will from Buck and onto his horse. "You all right?"

Will tried to move, but his fingers felt frozen. "I can't get my hands loose," he said between coughs. "They're caught in his mane." His teeth chattered with the cold rain. "I can't straighten my fingers."

"Dan!" Goodnight's voice boomed with the thunder. Lightning reflected off the wet backs of the confused, frightened horses as they lunged up the bank from the river. "Turn 'em toward camp. Naldo and the boys are coming for 'em."

"See Cookie's fire?" Pa showed Will the flickering light in a grove of trees. "Let the remuda go by, then head for camp. I'll be there when we settle these mounts." His horse leaped as his spurs raked its flanks, and he raced to turn the leaders.

"Pa!" Will called as the darkness sucked him up.

Buck shook his mane and pawed the ground.

"Whoa, Buck." Will strained to see, but the darkness consumed him.

"Pa just left us."

Water poured in dark streaks. His hat brim collapsed and funneled the cold rain down the back of his neck. The remuda flowed past like the roiling, tumbling river behind them. Will wanted to reach for the green ribbon, but his hands were still tangled in Buck's mane.

Thunder crashed, and lightning again lit the sky. In the flash of white light, Will saw Naldo and the drovers with Pa and the horse herd. A cramp gripped his left leg in a squeezing vice. He cried out and stretched his leg straight. The pain eased a little. The men moved the herd toward the rope corral, away from the noise and terror of the river.

When Will rode into camp, Jake threw a blanket around him. He untangled Buck's mane from Will's fingers. The shivering boy slid off his horse and pulled Buck under a corner of the tarp, which Cookie had strung from the cook wagon to some tree branches. He hobbled to the fire, sheltered from the rain, and rubbed the lingering pain from the cramp in his leg.

Pa rode in with Goodnight, Smokey, and Hank. They grabbed blankets and huddled around the warmth, taking sips of hot coffee.

Pa sat next to Will. "You all right, son?"

"Yes, Buck brought me to camp," he said without looking at Pa.

Cookie took a long stick and pushed up the center of the tarp. Water streamed off all four sides. Their roof sagged a little less.

One of the twins rubbed Will's hands and arms with the blanket.

"Thanks, Tony," Will said.

"I'm Tony," said the other twin as he refilled Will's coffee. "That's Jake."

Will looked from one grinning face to the other. "Aw, heck. I'll never learn which of you is which."

"Hank?" Will noticed the man's soggy mustache dripped as he sipped his hot coffee. "Did Curtis's spotted horse make it across? I saw him go under when that log hit him."

"He made it. They all made it. Some are pretty banged up, but nothing too serious."

Will stood and walked to Buck.

Pa followed him. "I'll take care of Buck. You stay by the fire."

"No. He's mine. I'll do it."

Pa turned him around. "What's the matter?"

"You left us, Pa. You left us in the dark. Buck brought me in."

Pa dropped his arm. "Dang it, Will. What's come over you? It's my job. I knew you would make it to camp. Anybody who could swim that river like you and Buck could find camp. You keep telling me you're grown up. Act like it."

Will watched Pa slip a halter on Buck. Dropping his eyes, he splashed his boot in a puddle and chewed his lip. *We did swim that river, and it was a bad one.* He looked back toward the roar of the swollen river. *We did it. And nobody helped us.*

Pa tied Buck to a wagon wheel and rubbed him with a blanket.

Will walked up to the wagon as Pa slipped the feed bag, with an extra handful of oats, over Buck's ears and rested his forehead on the wet shoulder.

"Thank you, again, for taking care of my boy."

Buck's ears twitched as he munched the grain.

Will walked to Pa and took the brush from his hand and started working the tangles from Buck's long tail.

"Pa?" Will pulled a twig from a tangle. "I sure didn't know Buck could swim so good."

Pa smiled and brushed the horse's coat smooth. "I didn't, either. You were doing a pretty good job yourself."

Will grinned.

Mr. Goodnight brought two cups of steaming coffee over. "Will, that horse can stay in camp and sleep in my blankets if he wants to. I'm not sure we could have saved those horses if he hadn't caused such a ruckus when you whistled. We didn't lose even one. Naldo has them settled in the rope corral with the others. They're acting like they never left home."

Will glanced at Pa's face, relieved to see only weariness. "Did you hear that, Buck? You can stay with me in camp." Will and Pa returned to the fire.

Goodnight filled the empty coffee cups of the drovers sitting around the campfire. "Men, get what sleep you can. Daylight is not far off, and we move out at first light." Goodnight grinned at the moans and groans that came from the tired riders.

Will took his bedroll and stretched out under the chuck wagon, out of the rain and near his best friend. He lay wrapped in his blankets and looked at the bottom of the wagon. Buck rubbed his head on the wheel and the wagon shook.

"Ya know what, Buck? I hope there are no more rivers like the Colorado. That was a mean stretch of water. I don't ever want to cross a river like that again." The thought of that cold, racing water made him shiver. "It sure did scare us, didn't it?" Will rolled toward him and propped himself on one elbow. "I didn't know you could swim that good. Is there anything you can't do?"

NORTH CONCHO RIVER

Will was not happy to see the sun rise. Lingering in his blankets seemed like a good idea, but he rolled out with the rest of the tired cowboys.

"Come on, Will-boy. Them critters won't wait for lazy drovers," remarked Curtis.

Will dragged himself, leading Buck to Naldo for his saddle.

About midmorning, he pulled Buck to a stop. The big horse cropped a few mouthfuls of prairie grass. Pa rode up. The cattle moved along slow and easy.

"There's one good thing about all the rain we had last night. There's no dust to kick up." Will slouched in the saddle, letting Buck graze as he ambled along. He pulled off his battered hat, rolled the brim for a tight grip, and fanned his hot face. "But it sure is muggy."

They rode in silence for a while.

"Pa, what's the North Concho like? It's not as bad as the Colorado, is it?"

Pa pulled the blade of grass he was chewing from his mouth. "You didn't like that crossing, did you?"

"No, I didn't."

"I didn't like it much myself. We won't cross any more big rivers. I can't promise anything about storms, but the North Concho is not anything like the Colorado." Pa grinned at him. "We should be there in three, maybe four days."

Goodnight hollered and motioned with his hat for Pa to come to the front of the herd.

"Turn Buck in with the remuda and ride with Cookie this afternoon."

"What for?" Will blurted out, surprised. "What did I do?"

"Nothin'. With Comanche in the area, I want you to stay close to the wagon. Cookie needs firewood for night camp, and you're just the one to get it for him. Anyway, Buck needs a rest."

Pa rode off at a lope.

Will sat and watched him. *We whipped the Comanche. They won't come around us again.* His stomach fluttered. He slipped his hand in his pocket and touched the green ribbon.

Pa caught up with Mr. Goodnight, and they disappeared ahead of the herd. Will didn't move. As he watched the herd move slowly past, he couldn't decide which bothered him more—his fear of the Comanche or his frustration at being tied to Cookie.

Rory popped a wandering steer to bring him in line. Will watched the older man. Callused hands swung the rope like it was an extension of the strong arms. The face of each drover who passed had tough lines and hard eyes. Strong muscles showed under their shirts. Will remembered Curtis saying what a crack shot Hank was, and he remembered seeing Russ shoot a rabbit from a running horse. His stomach stopped fluttering. *The Comanche won't come back.*

He remembered Cookie and the firewood. *I bet I've collected a whole forest of firewood on this drive. That's no job for a drover.* He slapped his leg with his hat, then jerked it down on his head. Buck turned an ear back. Will cut through a break in the line of slow plodding cattle to the opposite side of the herd.

"Cookie." He rode up alongside the mules that pulled the heavy wagon. "Pa said you needed firewood, but the sling under the wagon looks like it has some in it. So, you don't need me, right? I think Curtis needs me to help him on swing."

Will pulled the reins to turn Buck back to the herd.

"That's not enough wood to bake dried apple pies for supper. We're heading away from the river, so firewood is gettin' scarce. You need to fill that sling to the top. Get down off that horse and get after it."

Will reined up short and watched the wagon pull ahead. "Old goat." He slid off Buck, flipped the reins over the saddle horn, and walked after the wagon, picking up sticks. When his arms filled, he caught up with the wagon and tossed the wood in the canvas sling. Buck trailed behind, cropping the prairie grass and switching his long tail at flies.

"Cookie," Will called when he dumped the third armload of sticks. "Is that enough? Curtis needs me."

"Is it full?" Cookie's eyes never left the back ends of the wagon team.

"Sort of."

"Sort of won't do. Fill it up."

One hot day rolled into the next. Will picked up firewood and carried water from every creek they passed to pour in the water barrels.

The third morning, Will sat beside Curtis at breakfast.

"Cookie's treating me like a slave. If I carry any more water, my arms are gonna get stretched to the ground. Don't you need me to help you today?"

"Not today, Will-boy. Stay with Cookie." He flipped Will's hat to the ground and headed for the remuda.

Will put his hat back on and picked at his biscuit. *Pa won't let me ride with the herd. Curtis won't let me help him. Cookie thinks I'm his slave. All because of that Comanche.*

On the fourth day, Will carried water to the wash pan for Cookie to wash the morning dishes, but Cookie handed him the dishrag.

"Hurry up and wash these. I've got to hitch the team. If we make good time today, we can reach the North Concho by night camp."

Will looked at the dishrag in his hand, the pan of soapy water, and the stack of dirty dishes. His eyes blinked as fast as a hummingbird's wings.

"What?" The dishrag hit the ground. "In case you forgot, I'm a drover. I'm gonna find Pa. I need to talk to him."

"Come back here!" Cookie hollered.

Will looked back but didn't stop. He found Pa at the rope corral saddling his mount for the day.

"What are you doing here? You're supposed to be with Cookie." Pa reached under the horse and grabbed the cinch.

"Why can't I ride with the herd? That dang Cookie wants me to wash dishes. Drovers don't wash dishes."

Pa chuckled and pulled the cinch tight. "Drovers do the job they're assigned. You stay with Cookie. Do everything he tells you."

Will yanked off his hat and slapped his leg. "There aren't any Comanche near here. We ran them off. It's not fair. I'm a drover, not a camp swamper."

"You stay with Cookie. I don't want you riding around by yourself."

"You told me before we left not to worry about the Indians. Now, you're the one worrying."

"That was then. This is now."

Pa stepped into the stirrup and swung his leg over the saddle. He gave a final warning: "Stay with Cookie."

When Will loaded the crate of clean tin dishes in the wagon, some of the plates had new dents.

"Ya know what, Buck?" Will said as he followed the North Concho upriver, searching for a good fishing spot. "I don't mind helping Cookie when he needs me to go fishin'. Besides, I'm gettin' awful tired of beef and beans."

Nothing struck him as a likely hiding place for fish. Even though Cookie had told him to stay in sight of camp, he kept going. A quick glance back showed Cookie busy at the wagon. Riding Buck down the bank to the water, he followed the river for a quarter of a mile. They came to a pool near a grove of cottonwood trees. Willows trailed their long branches in the slow current and an old log lay half submerged in the water. Will dismounted and pulled his hook and string from his saddlebags. "I'm glad the drovers talked him into fish for tonight."

He took an empty tin can and an old flour sack Cookie had given him from his saddlebag and dug under the log. Soon his can was full of squirming brown earthworms. He stripped a long, thin willow branch of its leaves and tied his string to the end, making a perfect fishing pole.

He walked to the end of the log, plopped down, and pulled off his boots. The cool water swirled around his feet while he baited his hook and threw it into the pool. Dragonflies swooped and skimmed the surface of the water. Shadows from the trees danced and swayed with the gentle breeze.

The hook had barely sunk when his pole nearly jumped from his hands. He swung the end over his head. A catfish landed on the bank behind him. The flopping fish made it hard to pull his hook from its mouth. But it soon swam around in the flour sack, which hung in the water from a broken limb on the log.

"Did you see that? This pool is full of fish." He grinned as the horse raised his head, green grass hanging from his mouth, and looked at Will. "Stay close to the river," he warned as Buck moved slowly down the bank.

The flour sack filled as the afternoon wore on. The sun beat on Will, and sweat trickled down his back. Moving farther along the river, he came to a sandbar in a bend where the current had worn away the bank. The shallow water looked inviting.

"Ya know what, Buck? I just might go swimming after I catch a few more fish. I'm about to burn up." He stepped into the shade and fished under the draping branches of some willow trees. He watched Buck follow a trail away from the river to a small meadow where the grass was plentiful.

"Hey," Will called, "don't go too far." The horse twitched his ears.

Splash, another fish landed on the sandbar. "You can't get away from me," Will laughed and stuffed it in the flour sack. He looked back. "Buck?"

No call answered.

Will climbed up the bank from the sandbar and looked around. The empty meadow stretched to the edge of some woods. He followed the trail and found the buckskin grazing on the far side of the meadow. He headed across the clearing. Just as the horse lifted his head from the grass, a slim Indian, two feathers streaming from his hair, ran from the trees, grabbed the reins, and leaped into the saddle.

"Hey! What are you doing?" Will tore across the meadow.

Buck exploded into a frenzy of bucking. The Indian hung on. The big horse lowered his head and leaped into the air. The would-be thief landed on the ground.

Will threw himself at his enemy.

Buck circled the fighting pair, snorting and pawing the ground.

Will swung a solid right that connected with the Indian's jaw. They both scrambled to their feet. Buck rushed at the intruder, but he dove out of the way.

Catching Will around the waist, the Indian took him to the ground. Will grunted as the air whooshed from his lungs. They rolled and tumbled, stirring up clouds of dust. The Indian slugged Will on the jaw. The metallic taste of blood filled his mouth.

Will rolled away and leaped to his feet, spitting blood. He backed off as his opponent jumped up. They circled each other warily.

Buck pranced around the outside of their circle.

The Indian feinted with his right fist. Will jerked back, but a hard left to his stomach made him gasp and stagger.

Fury filled Will as the Indian sneered and said something in Comanche. They rushed each other, each landing solid hits. A fist connected with Will's eye, and pain exploded in his head.

He struck a blow that bloodied the Indian's lip. They stepped away. Both spit blood from split lips.

"You aren't gettin' my horse!" yelled Will.

Their eyes locked. Both boys moved cautiously, each watching the other. Will realized the Indian was not much older or bigger than he. "You aren't gettin' my horse," Will growled.

"Warrior's horse!" the Indian shouted.

"Will, where are you?" They both turned to the river at Cookie's call.

The Indian raced for the woods. Hoofbeats faded away.

"Cookie!" Will called. He grabbed Buck's reins and headed for the river, breathing heavily. The horse snorted at the smell of blood on Will's face. They met Cookie coming across the meadow.

"What happened to you?" Cookie reached for the boy's chin and turned his face to the light. "Look at that eye and lip! What a mess."

Will winced and pulled away. "That same Indian tried to ride off on Buck again." The horse snorted and jerked his head up and down. "Whoa, Buck." Will tugged on Buck's reins and patted the sweat-soaked neck. "Calm down."

"You mean the one you ran into in the canyon?" Cookie looked back and forth between Will and his horse.

"Yes. Buck threw him off. We fought, but he ran away when you called."

Cookie followed the tracks into the woods and found where the Comanche had tied his horse. Clear hoofprints showed where the horse had galloped off.

"You were supposed to fish near camp. You know that Indian's been following the herd. Dan is not going to be happy about this."

"I told Pa I didn't want to stay in camp anymore. There weren't any fish there. I had to go where the fish were." Will cocked his head to see Cookie out of the one eye not swollen shut. "Do we have to tell him about the fight?"

"No, we don't have to tell him, but I think he'll figure it out."

Buck followed them to the river and dipped his muzzle in the water and drank.

Cookie pulled his bandana from his pocket and gave it to Will. "Tell me what happened."

Will knelt at the river's edge and bathed his split lip and swollen eye while he told the older man about the fight. Buck drank again.

"Cookie." The swelling in his lip made it difficult to talk.

The old man took the bandana. Will let the gnarled hands gently wipe the blood off his face.

"You know what? Smokey's right. He is just a kid. Not much older'n me and not much bigger. Buck and me whupped him good. We'll whup him the next time, too. He's not gettin' my horse."

"Let's get back to camp. Dan and Charlie need to hear about this." Cookie picked up the flour sack full of fish. Will pulled on his socks and boots. They headed for camp.

Pa took one look at Will's split lip and swollen eye, listened to his story, and, with a grim look, saddled his horse. The trail boss walked up and handed Dan a bridle.

"That's three times, Charlie. I can't risk Will having another encounter with that Indian, boy or not. I'm goin' after him."

Charlie Goodnight turned to the men gathered around Will. "Hank, you and Russ go with Dan," Goodnight said. "It's a while before dark. See if you can track him. He may lead you to the ones that stole our horses. Maybe you'll find their camp." The boss started to walk away, but turned back. "Dan, if there's a lot of them, come back, and I'll send more with you. The rest of you boys, double the guard. If there's Comanche in the area, I don't want to take any chances of them getting to the herd or the remuda again."

"Stay in camp while I'm gone, son," Pa told Will, his hand gently squeezing the boy's shoulder. "I'll be back in a few days."

"Yes, sir." Suddenly, Will was afraid for Pa. What if there were a whole bunch of Comanche? What if something happened to Pa because he hadn't obeyed orders? What if Pa didn't come back? "Come back safe, Pa."

Pa nodded. Will let go of the reins, and he rode away.

As they came into camp for dinner, each drover bragged on the size of Will's swollen lip and made bets on the shades of black-and-blue his eye would turn by morning. The slab of raw meat Cookie gave him to put on his eye did little to reduce the swelling. The fight grew more thrilling, and the Indian's defeat grew worse, each time Will told the story.

Even their concern over his fight didn't hinder the men's appetites as they savored the hot, crunchy fried fish. They ate quickly and headed back out to the herd. The news of Will's fight, and that Comanche might be nearby, soon spread to the drovers still with the herd.

The salty fish stung Will's split lip, but he managed to eat his fill. He made sure he tied Buck firmly to a wagon wheel.

The sense of unease that lay over the camp made Will nervous. *Where are the Comanche? Where is Pa?*

OLD PONY

Two Feathers raced from the meadow. His split lip dripped blood, and his sore ribs pounded with every step. Disappointment lay heavily on him. *If only the old man had not come. I beat the white boy. The dunnia was mine.* He grit his teeth against the pain and swung a leg over Old Pony. Kicking his horse into a gallop, he made quick time to his camp and packed his things. As he broke camp, he kept his eyes focused on his back trail. He tied his pack on the horse, slipped his bow and quiver on his back, and pointed Old Pony south toward the next river. He swung wide away from the herd and kicked him into a fast lope.

"The whites will come to find us," he said to Old Pony. "I know you are tired, but we have no time for rest."

Two Feathers and Old Pony traveled late into the night. He used every trick he knew to hide his trail. He stayed away from game trails, where the horse's tracks might show. He used clumps of grass or a leafy branch to wipe out tracks when they did make them. At a creek crossing, Old Pony stepped on the muddy bank, and Two Feathers stopped long enough to scatter dirt, twigs, and broken leaves to cover the track. The need to get farther from the whites burned like a festering sore in his mind. If he could only remember all the ways Comanche warriors hid tracks.

Old Pony's hooves mashed down the prairie grass. He worried it would not spring back in time to hide his passage. The moon's bright light helped him find rocky trails that left fewer tracks. He stayed under the shelter of trees whenever he could and stuck to the draws and arroyos, away from hills and ridges where he would be outlined against the moonlight.

The trail behind him remained empty as the hours passed. Old Pony faltered and stumbled over a small boulder, hitting his left front hoof hard. Two Feathers sat up. He had slumped in the saddle and dozed.

"We need to camp." He patted the old horse on the neck. The dark outline of trees loomed in the distance. "There." A dry creek bed wound its way through the trees, and Two Feathers found a cutout under a high bank. He slid to the ground and picked up a fallen branch. He pushed and jabbed the stout stick into the cutout. Satisfied no badger or skunk lived there, he unsaddled Old Pony. A little water remained in his water pouch, and using his cup, he poured it into Old Pony's mouth, saving a swallow for himself. Some of the precious water dribbled out over his numb and swollen lip.

As he hobbled Old Pony to keep him close, he whispered to his friend. "I need some willow tea but cannot risk a fire. The whites might see it. You stay close. There is some dried grass in the creek bed and some leaves on the tree branches. You will have to make do with that. When we are far away, I will find you good grass."

He spread one of his sleeping skins out flat in the cutout. Crawling in on top of it, he wiggled the other one over him.

He barely fit. A piece of jerked venison provided him supper. His jaw hurt too much to chew, so he sucked on it until it softened enough to swallow.

The pulsing song of the cicada hummed and faded, hummed and faded, until his worry eased and sleep emptied his mind.

A cramp in Two Feathers's leg made him sit straight up with a yelp, banging his head on the roof of the cutout. He stretched his leg outside his sleeping hole, and the cramp let go. Propping himself on one elbow and rubbing his leg, he looked around for Old Pony. He spotted a dark shape in the shadows near the oak trees. The horse stood with its head drooped and one back leg tipped up on its hoof, fast asleep.

Two Feathers smiled. "Sleep, my old friend. You worked hard today." He snuggled back under his sleeping skin, wishing the cutout was long enough to stretch out his curled-up legs.

First light found Two Feathers and Old Pony heading southwest. Yesterday, he had set his sights on the setting sun, but today he thought again of the dunnia. There had been no sign of any followers. He once again set out for the cattle herd. Confidence in his ability to hide his tracks made him smile. *Barks Like Coyote thinks he is a great warrior. He is no warrior. Brave men ride with him. They tell him where to go and what to eat. No one tells me. I am the strong one. I ride alone.*

The hot sun burned from a cloudless sky. Trees and other objects in the distance wavered and shimmered with the late morning heat. Two Feathers's throat burned. His tongue felt sticky. He wished he had drunk more sparingly that morning.

Old Pony stopped. Two Feathers slid off and led his friend in a slow walk. Up ahead, a dark shape appeared in the haze.

It grew as they approached. *Trees. Maybe water.* Old Pony perked up and quickened his pace.

"Water? Do you smell water?"

A row of trees wound to the southwest. They rushed into the trees and found a dry creek bed. Rocks and weeds choked the watercourse.

Two Feathers knelt and began to dig. A stout stick helped him push rocks out of the way. The dirt was damp. He grinned and dug deeper. The ground became wet. At elbow depth, he lined the hole with rocks. He used long bunches of grass to clean most of the mud from his arms and hands.

"We will have water before the sun moves far across the sky." Once again, he hobbled Old Pony. "You will not go far from the smell of the water, but we will be careful."

Before he sat down to rest, he checked his back trail for followers. A puff of dust blew up in the distance, then disappeared. Nothing more showed. "Only a swirling wind," he decided. *I think we are safe. I am a warrior. They will not find me.*

Even the rough bark of the oak tree he leaned against could not keep him awake. The sun crested and started its slow decent. The hum of cicadas lulled him to sleep.

Old Pony nickered. Two Feathers jerked awake. *Horses.* He stood and placed a warning hand on Old Pony's muzzle and found it wet. Two Feathers glanced at his hole in the creek bed. It held water.

A hoof clinked against stone. Two Feathers eased up the slope from the creek bed and risked a sweeping look over the prairie. *White men.* His breath stuck in his chest.

Three riders walked their horses toward him. Dizziness blurred his vision and made him sick. Their voices rang clear in the hot air. He froze. *How did they find me?*

One pointed to the ground, then straight at the spot where Two Feathers hid. In a panic, he slid down the slope with a clatter of rocks, leaves, and sticks that seemed to echo through the trees like the screeching of a flock of crows. He threw a longing glance at the water in the hole and leaped on Old Pony. The white men raced after him down the dry creek bed and up onto the prairie. He heard the pounding of hooves behind him and the shout of voices.

Two Feathers kicked Old Pony into full gallop, but the old horse could not hold out against the stronger horses of the white men. Ropes hissed like snakes when they encircled Two Feathers and jerked him to the ground. Air exploded from his lungs. He rolled to his knees, then staggered to his feet. The ropes stretched tight, one on each side, and burned his chest and arms. He could not move. Anger roared in his ears. He lunged forward and backward and side-to-side, but the white men's horses backed away, keeping the ropes taut.

He stopped. *I am Comanche. Be still. Be strong.* He took a deep breath. The trembling in his legs threatened to drop him, so he stiffened his knees and rolled his toes in his moccasins.

He looked at the white men. First one. Then the second. Then the third. This one's rope held Old Pony. The old horse's eyes showed white and rolled in fear. He pulled against the rope, moving in a circle away from the man.

Gasps of air rushed hard into Two Feathers's already dry mouth. He spat blood from a bit lip. Shifting his weight from leg to leg helped his circulation, and his head cleared. He looked at Old Pony. "Be still, old friend. You are not hurt."

Two Feathers's words calmed the horse, but still he strained against the ropes, not liking the strange horses or the scent of the white men.

"Be still. We will see what these white men do." He didn't know if his words were to calm Old Pony or himself.

The third white man spoke to the others and led Old Pony back to the creek bed. The others moved their horses closer to Two Feathers, shortening the ropes holding him. They walked him back to the water hole. Two Feathers longed for a drink, even though it looked muddy.

The white man spoke to the others and nodded—first in the captive's direction, then toward the water. The ropes loosened enough for Two Feathers to kneel and drink his fill.

The white men dismounted and tied Two Feathers's hands and feet. They dropped him at the base of a tree. He sat up and leaned against the rough bark.

A prisoner, he thought. *I am their prisoner.* A vision of a captive that Yellow Hawk had once brought into their village after a raid caused a spasm like knife pricks—as many as the stars in the sky—to flash over his body. He remembered the treatment given to that Apache warrior. *I must get away.* The sweat that soaked his body did not come from the late-August heat. He fought his fear. *Slow deep breaths. Air in slow. Air out slow. Air in slow. Air out slow.* He repeated this mantra over and over until his fear settled to a level he thought he could control.

The men unsaddled their horses. The lanky third man gathered sticks and dried grass to start a fire. Having seen these men only from a long distance while he watched the dunnia, he studied them. One of them must be the boy's father. Not the one with the hair on his lip. Not the one with the wide shoulders and thick arms. His eyes kept returning to the lanky, sandy-haired man. That face showed an older, stronger version of the boy he had fought.

The long, hot afternoon passed. The white men took turns resting and keeping watch. The tall man brought him water in a tin cup. The water slid down his throat. He drank eagerly.

He listened and began to understand some of what they said. This surprised him. Many summers had passed since the day of death. He no longer even thought in the white man's words. Yellow Hawk had not allowed him to speak the white tongue. So he had forgotten it.

The man with hair on his lip built up the fire and began to cut some kind of meat into strips and cook it. Two Feathers did not recognize the meat, but his nose did. He sniffed.

Mother cooked meat like this. I remember she called it bacon. She would not let me have any until it cooled. She wrapped it in bread and gave it to me. My father loved it and ate many pieces.

The tall man untied his hands long enough for Two Feathers to eat the bacon and drink water from the hole in the creek bed, then retied them. They kept Old Pony tied to a stout tree branch, but they took him to drink. Old Pony began to lose his nervousness around the white men.

Two Feathers's arms and shoulders ached, and his wrists burned from the rough ropes. He twisted his hands and tried to roll his shoulders to relieve them, but nothing helped. He sat with his back against the tree and watched. The tall man spoke to him. Even though the words had a familiar sound, he could not make them out. He simply stared at him. *I am Comanche. I am strong,* he thought each time the white man spoke.

Late in the afternoon, they broke camp. Two of the whites untied Two Feathers's feet, then picked him up by his arms and put him on Old Pony. *Where do they take me? Why have they not killed me?*

The tall man led Old Pony and carried Two Feathers's pack, quiver, and bow behind his saddle. Two Feathers gripped his horse with his thighs to keep his balance. The rested horses moved at a steady lope back the way they had come. The hours he and the other young boys had spent riding, with only their knees guiding their horses, kept him in the saddle.

They rode till dusk and made a dry camp. Again, the smell of cooking bacon brought back memories of the cabin and his white father. More of the white man's words slipped into his mind.

"Give this to the boy."

Two Feathers looked up in surprise that he knew the words. The stout man with strong arms handed the tall one some bacon.

The tall man looked at the captive. "You understand English?"

Two Feathers dropped his head and would not answer. He ate the bacon.

Dark slipped into the camp. Their small fire burned down to a glowing bed of coals. The tall man rolled in his blanket away from the heat. The one with hair on his lip sat for a while, sipping from a cup, then settled on his blanket. The moon hung overhead. Its pale light left shadows moving over the sleeping whites. A coyote howled to the full moon, and the stout man walked away from camp to settle the nervous horses.

Two Feathers finally slipped one raw hand from the rough ropes and shook it to restore circulation. He rubbed the other and untied his ankles. The stout man returned from the horses, and Two Feathers put his hands behind him. He did not move. His head drooped. He watched from half-closed eyes. The man moved away from camp, and his footsteps stopped about twenty yards out.

Two Feathers eased to his feet. He stood still until he could trust his legs to hold him. Then he moved silently to his things and to Old Pony. He had been tied away from the other horses and stood still while saddled. Two Feathers led him a distance from camp, then mounted and walked away from the whites. He eased out of the clump of trees and onto the open prairie. *Whites,* he thought. *They sleep too sound and do not listen to the night. Yellow Hawk would have killed all of them.* That thought made him shiver. Suddenly, he did not want the whites harmed. *The tall man is like my father. He is good to his son.*

A rope hissed through the bright moonlight. Two Feathers hit the ground hard. Old Pony trotted away, stopped, and looked back, confused.

"You aren't going anywhere, boy. You're staying with us till we reach the herd and then all the way to the soldiers at Fort Sumner."

The stout man stepped from the shadows of a lone tree and pulled Two Feathers to his feet and back to camp. Old Pony followed.

MIDDLE CONCHO RIVER

Will slipped away from Cookie and rode Buck out onto the prairie to watch for Pa. *How far can that Indian run in three days? Where is Pa?* He had headed around the herd to check with the drovers on the other side when Curtis caught up with him.

"Cookie's madder than a nest of hornets. You better get back to camp."

"He's worse than an old lady." Will turned Buck back toward the chuck wagon. "What's taking Pa so long?" He picked at a callus on his finger and looked up at Curtis. "Why isn't he back?"

"I don't know. But you better stay in camp like your Pa said, or Cookie is gonna have a fit."

Will tied Buck to the wagon wheel, walked over to the pile of pecans waiting for him, and threw himself on the ground. He picked up his hammer from the mound of broken shells. His lip, raw from three days of nervous chewing on it and still sore from the fight, protested when he bit into it, so he rubbed it with his tongue. *Whack,* another pecan split open. He pried the nutmeat from its shell with his pocketknife and added it to a small pile. The shade from the huge pecan tree cooled the gentle breeze that blew from the Middle Concho River near camp. He looked at the slowly shrinking pile of unshelled pecans and sighed.

Honey Allen, a short man with long yellow hair who dressed in buckskins and traded in honey and pecans, grinned at Will. The man's legs stretched out in front of him as he leaned against the trunk of the pecan tree. The sound his knife made as he dragged it across a whetstone grated on Will's ears. Will looked at the man's worn boots and stained clothes and wondered how he traveled all around without the Comanche getting him. Allen had come into camp that morning from down south on the Devil's River. Mr. Goodnight bought jugs of honey and a tow sack full of pecans from him.

Cookie frowned at Will's small pile of nuts as he walked back up from the river with a bucket of water. "You'll be happy you shelled them when you taste my dried apple pecan cobbler after supper tonight."

"That's right, Will-boy," Curtis said as he followed Cookie into camp with a second bucket of water. "Cookie makes a fine cobbler."

"Isn't this enough? Some of these nuts aren't very good." Will showed Cookie a dry, shriveled nutmeat. A picture of a golden pie cooling on the kitchen table of their cabin flashed across his mind. *I bet his cobbler's not as good as Ma's pecan pie.* Will looked away from Cookie.

"These are last year's nuts," Honey Allen answered. "Look up yonder in this big ol' tree. It's plum full of pecans, but they won't be ready for another couple of months. I'll be back this way then. It looks like I'll find plenty."

"No, it's not enough," Cookie said after a glance at Will's pile. "Keep workin'."

"Where do you keep these here pecans?" Curtis asked Mr. Allen. "They're mighty fresh to be near a year old." The cowboy sat next to Allen and rested his back against the tree, tipped his hat to the back of his head, and crossed his ankles. A scattering of shavings collected on his lap as he whittled on a small figure of a horse.

"I got me a hidey-hole down south of here a ways. The cave stays dry and cool year-round. The rains last spring and early summer made for a good crop. I store my extras down there where it's cool enough for 'em to keep."

"Where is this hidin' place?" Curtis grinned at the old man.

"Now, that's my little secret, cowboy. It's come in mighty handy a few times when I had to hide from some not-too-friendly Comanche."

Curtis winked at Will and whittled on his horse.

Worry about Pa dug furrows in Will's forehead. *I'm sick of Cookie, camp, and Curtis. If I can get to the herd, I'll slip away and go find Pa.*

Will popped a pecan in his mouth. "Cookie, I know Pa said I had to stay in camp, but that Indian ain't around here. I want to get back to the herd. They need me."

"You're just fine right here. We're takin' a few days to let the herd fill up on grass and water, so those cows aren't going anywhere. Besides, Mr. Goodnight told you to stay in camp till Dan gets back."

"Pa's been gone for three days. Do ya think something happened to him?"

"Don't you worry, Will-boy." Curtis lifted the carving to the light and shaved a thin slice off one ear. "Your Pa is about as good a tracker and frontiersman as there is. He'll come back to you safe and sound."

Will cracked another pecan with his hammer and picked out the nutmeat. He wiped the sweat off his face with his bandana. A fly buzzed around his head. He swatted at it. *We're just sittin' here. Waitin'. If we were moving, Pa wouldn't have so far to come back.*

"Why'd we stop here, anyway? It's just gettin' hotter and hotter." Will slapped at a fly on his leg. "Why can't we just go on? We won't ever get to New Mexico if we keep stoppin'. I'm sick of being in camp. Why don't you tell Mr. Goodnight to just go?"

Cookie stood from stirring the stew on the cook fire. "Now you listen here. In the first place, I don't tell Mr. Goodnight anything, and in the second place, I don't have to listen to your complaining. Get busy and crack them nuts."

"Boy," said Honey Allen, "this next stretch of trail between here and Horsehead Crossing is a real killer. There's nothin' but hot sun and alkali dust. Not a drop of water for three days." He reached for his canteen and took a deep swallow. "You drink all the water you can, or you won't last the trip. Charlie Goodnight knows what he's doin' by keeping the herd here. These cattle need all the grass and water they can hold. That's a mean crossing. I don't like making it by myself. I remember one time when I crossed the Pecos—"

"I'd better go see to Buck." Will jumped up. "He's not gettin' enough to eat or drink."

"Will," said Cookie. "Sit down. Buck is just fine. He's gettin' plenty of grass and water."

Will slumped back down and picked up his hammer. *Whack!* He smashed a pecan flat.

"Whoa, boy," laughed Honey Allen. "Give me that hammer. I'll crack some for a while. I remember one time on the Pecos I run into a bunch of Comanche. If I hadn't had a wagon full of honey and pecans, I'd have lost my hair for sure. Them durn Indians took half my load. I did trade for some fine buffalo hides, though, so I guess I made out all right."

Tony and Jake came up from the river, their arms full of fresh-washed clothes and blankets. They draped them over the low tree limbs and shrubs to dry.

"What are you doin' there, Will-boy?" asked one of the twins.

"Aw, Jake, they've got me shelling pecans when I need to be with the herd."

"I'm Tony, that's Jake," Tony said, pointing to his brother.

"Why don't you guys dress different so a person knows who he's talking to?" Will grinned at the twins, then turned serious. "Have you guys seen any sign of Pa? He's been gone a long time."

"No, not yet," Jake said.

"I 'spect he'll be in 'fore too much longer," Tony said.

"Why don't you boys take Will down to the river and see if you can dig up some mussels?" Cookie nodded toward the river. "He's tired of shelling pecans. Mussels cooked with wild onions would taste pretty good."

"Yee-haw! Let's go," Jake hollered. He grabbed a bucket and his rifle and headed for the water.

Tony grabbed Will, threw him over his shoulder, picked up his rifle, and followed Jake.

"Let me down," yelled Will as he bobbed up and down. Tony's shoulder jabbed him in the stomach with every step.

"Down you go." Tony laughed as he dumped Will in the shallow water at the river's edge.

Will scrambled up and splashed to the bank. "What did you do that for?" He sat down beside the twins.

They pulled off their boots, rolled up their pant legs, and waded in.

Tony and Jake showed Will how to find the mussels and pull them from the rocks on the bottom of the river. The cold water numbed Will's feet as he searched for the biggest mussels. He found a big one and pulled it from the rocky bottom and dropped it in his bucket.

"Hey, look at this one," he called to one of the twins, bent over digging in mud under the rocks. As the drover looked up, Will scooped up a double handful of water and shot it at his face. "You're Tony, aren't you?" He ducked as water shot back at him.

"Yep, how'd you figure me out?"

Will squirted another shot of water. "You have a scar on the side of your neck just above your shirt collar and Jake don't."

"That's pretty good." Tony dodged the water, scooped up another handful, and shot it at Will. "I fell out of a tree when I was a youngster and cut it on a branch on the way down. You gonna tell everybody?"

Will's jump was a little slow, and the water caught him in the face. "Nope," he laughed. "I won't give away your secret."

"Hey, I'm not going to dig these mussels by myself. Quit yappin' and get busy." Jake smacked the river and water shot toward the pair.

After a while, Will stood to stretch his aching back. He noticed one of the twin's rifles lay nearby on the bank of the river and only one hunted for mussels at a time. The other kept his rifle in his hands and his eyes on the land beyond. Will looked back and forth between the men.

"Jake, what's going on?" He waded over and picked up a rifle.

"Now, Will." Tony took the gun. "We're just keepin' our eyes peeled for bears. One might decide to help himself to our mussels."

"Bears? Are you nuts? There ain't no bears here." Will's eyes didn't leave the Winchester in Tony's hands. "Pa said he would get me my own rifle when I'm twelve. That's not too far off. Ma made him promise to wait till then."

"Well, you know how mothers are." Tony grinned.

"You're watching for that Comanche, aren't you?" Will's voice rose in pitch. He cleared his throat and sucked in a long, slow breath. "I'm not afraid. I beat him once. I can beat him again."

With their bucket full, they pulled on their boots and began to search the area for any remaining wild onions.

"I don't see any onions around here." Will stood with his hands on his hips and looked around.

"They're not going to jump up at you. It's summer. The tops are dried. You have to look close to find any." Tony ran his hand through some tall dried grass.

Will and the twins moved up and down the riverbank. Will spent more time looking out across the prairie than at the ground. Tony and Jake found a few dried stalks and dug up the bulbs.

The sound of horses coming made them hurry back to camp. They arrived in time to see Pa, Hank, and Russ ride in, leading an old pony carrying an Indian boy with his hands tied.

"Pa!" Will called as the tired man stepped from his saddle. He ran to him and grabbed his hand. "You're back."

Pa laughed. "What have you been doing? You're soaking wet."

"Diggin' mussels," Will answered. "You got him!"

Hank untied the prisoner's hands, and Two Feathers staggered a little when he slid to the ground. Dirt streaked his still-battered face. The ropes left raw red bands around his wrists.

Will walked over to him. Standing not much taller than Will, the corners of his mouth twitched in a smirk.

Fury covered Will like a swarm of bees. He let out a wild yell and threw himself on the captive. They hit the ground. His fists connected with Two Feathers's nose and blood gushed.

Two Feathers scrambled away and leaped up, clenching his fists.

The boys lunged at each other.

"That's enough of that," yelled Russ as he and Hank each grabbed a pair of flailing arms and held the squirming, kicking boys.

"Will!" barked Pa. "Stop that! What's got into you?"

"He tried to get Buck! I whupped him once. I can whup him again."

"I beat you," growled the captive boy.

All action stopped. All eyes looked at the boy, astonished.

"You speak English?" Pa asked.

Two Feathers nodded.

The boys glared at each other.

Mr. Goodnight rode into camp and tied the grullo to a tree limb. "What's going on here? I saw you ride in with a prisoner." He looked at the captive. "What happened to him?" He gave Russ a stern look. "We don't treat boys that way."

"I didn't do this, boss."

Goodnight glanced at Will. "Russ, take him to the river and clean him up. I'm sure he needs a drink. Then see he gets plenty of food. He's thin as a rail."

Still holding tight to the boy's arms, Russ hauled him to the river. The Indian's eyes swept over the grullo as they walked past and lingered briefly on the deep chest and the stout legs. Russ stood watch as the boy drank.

Goodnight turned to Will. "No more fighting, you understand me?"

Will looked at his father. Pa nodded. Will turned back to Mr. Goodnight. "Yes, sir."

Smokey walked into camp and dropped his saddle and saddlebags on the ground. "What's going on?" Smokey asked.

"Dan caught the Indian boy that's been trailing the herd and trying to get Will's horse. He looks to be half white, even speaks some English. Russ has him at the river. See what you can find out about him."

Russ brought the captive over to the cook fire and ladled some stew on a plate. The Indian took it, sat on the ground, and began to scoop the hot stew into his mouth with his fingers. Smokey spoke to him in Comanche. The answers came between mouthfuls of stew.

Will, Dan, and Mr. Goodnight stood near and watched. The boy emptied the first plate and Smokey filled it again. They talked for a long time. The only words Will understood were *John Randall*. When the scout said those words, the Indian nodded. Smokey dropped the plate in the wash bucket and turned to Dan and Mr. Goodnight.

"He's half white, all right. His pa was John Randall. You remember him, Charlie?"

"Yes, didn't he live in Indian Territory?" Charlie asked. "I think he married a Comanche woman from Quanah Parker's band. If I remember right, they had a little spread along the Red River. He disappeared sometime before the war." Goodnight looked at the Indian. "So, this is his boy? What happened to his folks?"

"He's been living with his uncle, Yellow Hawk. Randall had brought his wife to visit her family when soldiers raided the village. They killed the boy's mother. He says Yellow Hawk killed his father. Says Yellow Hawk is now his enemy, so he ran away."

"Yellow Hawk. I remember that name. Isn't he a war chief?"

"He is. And a mean one. He raided along the Red River and into Northern Texas before the war. I understand he's moved south, somewhere on the Llano Estacado."

Will looked at the Indian slumped by the fire with his arms wrapped around his legs and his head resting on his knees. *His pa and ma are both dead.* He stared at Two Feathers. *Both of them.*

Two Feathers's head lifted. He smirked at Will, tapped his chest, and nodded. Will's fists clenched. *I won't let him get Buck. I won't.*

That night at dinner, Mr. Goodnight called the drovers, except the ones riding night herd, around the campfire. Will stood beside Pa. "Tomorrow we'll start for Horsehead Crossing. I'll tell you straight, it's going to get bad. There's no water. Nothing but heat and eighty miles of alkali dust."

He turned to Dan. "We'll push them day and night. No stopping." The ramrod nodded agreement.

"Each man guard your canteen. Use it sparingly. Cookie, fill everything that will hold water. Cook up enough biscuits to last till we get to the Pecos."

His eyes searched the stern faces before him. "Naldo?"

"Sí, I am here." The wiry wrangler stepped from the shadows.

"The men will need to change horses often. Keep the remuda as close to the herd as you can."

"Do not worry, I'll drive the remuda near the chuck wagon."

"Men, don't let your mounts get overtired. I know we'll lose cattle, but let's try to keep the horse loss to a minimum. Cookie, pack up camp and be ready to move at first light. Smokey, keep that Indian boy with you. We'll turn him over to the army when we get to Fort Sumner."

Will headed for the chuck wagon to get his bedroll. As he passed the captive, he kicked dirt on him. The Indian leaped to his feet. Smokey put a hand on the boy's shoulder. Will kept walking.

The trail boss's words, *It's going to get bad,* rang in his head. *Just how bad can it be? We've made dry camps before. Cookie's got lots of water barrels. So what could happen?*

EIGHTY MILES

First light found the drovers saddled and headed to the herd. Each cowboy carried a full canteen.

"Dan," said Charlie as Pa and Will rode up, "you two start at point with me. As the day heats up and they get thirsty, it's going to be hard to keep 'em pointed in the right direction."

"Ho, cattle, ho," shouted the drovers, slapping their lariats against their tough leather chaps. Once more, the longhorns lunged to their feet. Dan, Will, and Mr. Goodnight pointed the herd west toward the dry, trackless desert of the Staked Plains of Southwest Texas.

Ol' Blue took his place in the front. The flank and swing riders squeezed the cattle into a long line. The drag riders shoved and pushed the lazy ones to catch up. The herd was well away from the Middle Concho before sunrise.

"Will," Pa said, "your river of cattle is on the move again. I just hope this river doesn't shrink to a stream by the time we cross the Pecos."

"What do you mean?" Will asked.

"These beeves aren't going to have anything to eat or drink for the next three days but alkali dust and catclaw."

"What's alkali dust?"

"A kind of salt. Kills the grass. Poisons the water. This land has lots of it."

Will watched Pa jump his horse after a stray. *Pa sure makes it sound bad.*

The orange in the clouds faded to an amber glow as the sun appeared, warm on Will's shoulders and chasing away the chill of the desert night. It soon wore out its welcome and sweat began to trickle down Will's back.

He looked around. A patch of green here—prickly pear cactus. A patch of green there—jimsonweed. He looked due west. No green trees showed in the distance. No prairie grass waved in the wind. He picked up his canteen from where it hung on the saddle horn and shook it. The water sloshed inside. The sound made him thirsty, but he decided to wait a while before he took a drink.

"Buck, Pa may be right. I don't like this land. I don't know why we're here."

The morning dragged on. The sun bore down on cattle and men. Bitter alkali dust hung in the air and coated the faces of the drovers. They pulled their bandanas over their mouths and noses. Will's eyes burned and watered. His sweat felt like bugs crawling down his face.

Cookie stopped the chuck wagon at noon, and from a bucket of water the men wet their bandanas and wiped their horses' muzzles and mouths. Each horse got a small drink when the drovers changed to a fresh mount. From another bucket, Russ gave each man half a canteen of water.

Jake handed him his. "Boy," Russ growled, "this canteen is empty. You shouldn't of drunk it all this morning. Now, you'll have to make do on half a canteen. Learn to pace yourself."

Will rode up to the chuck wagon with Pa. He couldn't re-member ever being so hot. He wet his bandana. Buck reached for it, wanting the dampness. Will poured Buck's small share into a bucket. The horse sucked it dry. He pushed at Will, wanting more. Will looked around and, seeing no one watch-ing, slipped his canteen off the saddle and poured half into the bucket.

"Sorry, Buck. That's all I can give you."

Will led him over to Naldo and turned him in with the rest of the remuda.

With few words, drovers ate a hurried plate of cold biscuits with beef, gravy, and only one cup of coffee.

Each rode a fresh mount back to the herd. Will felt strange not riding Buck. Naldo had put him on a black horse with one white stocking. They plodded alongside the herd. The hours dragged. The sun seemed to be stuck in one spot.

Will pulled his hat low against the hot sun that burned his face. It burned his head through his hat, his back through his shirt, his legs through his pants. He felt woozy and dozed in the saddle.

Suddenly, the black jumped after a steer that turned from the herd. Will grabbed the saddle horn to keep from spilling off.

Curtis rode up. "Hey there, Will-boy. You better pay atten-tion. That black doesn't need to be told what to do. He'll leave you sittin' in the dust if you don't watch out."

"He just about did," Will grinned at the dust-coated cow-boy.

Men, horses, and cattle made their way through the long, hot afternoon. Will noticed his shadow had finally length-ened. He stopped so the black could rest and watched the herd as it stretched across the desert. *I wish I was home. The water from our well would sure taste good about now.*

Rory rode up and pulled his tired mount next to Will. "You better clean your horse's mouth and muzzle."

Will slid to the ground, pulled off his bandana, and wet it from his canteen. He wiped its nose and wet its tongue.

"You want to know something funny, Rory?"

"Sure do. Somethin' funny would be good about now." Rory grinned and scrubbed his sweat-soaked bandana over his face.

"We look like a bunch of robbers with bandanas covering our faces. I sure hope the Texas Rangers don't come along and think we stole this herd."

"Before this drive is over, we just might wish we had a passel of them Rangers."

"What do you mean?"

"The Comanche come through here." Rory tied his bandana around his neck. "The land west of the Pecos is Apache country. I'd sure like to see some of those Texas boys about now." Rory boosted Will back into the saddle.

"Ya know what, Blackie?" Will asked his horse as he watched the cowboy ride off. "I got a Comanche in camp that wants to steal my horse. We're heading into Apache country. And there's no water. I don't see how things could get much worse."

Will and the men rotated around the herd, pushing and shoving the thirsty cattle forward. Their loud bawling became hoarse squeaks as the dry day went on.

Clouds of white dust engulfed man and beast as they worked to keep the lagging cattle moving. Will couldn't see the men riding drag through the thick alkali fog. Mr. Goodnight ordered that position changed every two hours. The weaker cattle had to be pushed hard to stay up with the herd. Cows got separated from their calves and stopped to bawl. Dust covered everything. It sifted down Will's back and through his clothes. The itch tormented him. All he could think about was the little water left in his canteen.

The black horse stopped. Will watched the short-cropped mane waggle back and forth as the sweat-soaked horse shook his head. The saddle felt hard and stiff. His back ached. He stood in the stirrups, stretched, and rubbed his sore backside. Sweat trickled from under his hat. He pulled it off and ran his hand through his wet hair. He twisted the hat in his hands. "You're a mess." The hat made a soggy thud as he slapped it against his leg. "Blast that ol' rattlesnake for choosing my good hat to get in out of the sun."

"Will!" shouted Curtis. "Get a move on, boy. This ain't no place to stop."

Will jumped at Curtis's call. Jolted from his hot stupor, he nudged his horse after a steer that had also stopped. He looked around. No trees or green anywhere. Only greasewood shrubs and thorny catclaw that scratched at his chaps broke the unending monotony of the desert. Bitter dust coated his lips and burned his throat. He wiped the sweat from his face and his stinging eyes.

The black stopped again. Will pulled the stopper from his canteen and drank the last swallow. The warm, almost hot water tasted of metal and did little to ease his thirst. He remembered his mother's Big Dipper story. *I guess the Big Dipper tipped and spilled all its water because this traveler sure isn't getting any.*

At dusk, Pa and Will came off drag and rode their weary horses to the remuda to get fresh mounts.

"Don't you think Buck's rested enough?" Will asked Pa. "I think he's okay to ride now."

"I'm sure he is, but you're not. Cookie's set up supper camp. It looks like he's got food ready. Go get a drink, eat, and find a spot in the wagon. You need to sleep. It's been a long day."

"But no one else is going to bed." Will looked at his father. "I can ride. I can do it."

"I'm sure you can, Will. But I need you to stay in the wagon at night. I don't have time to worry about you."

"But, Pa. It's not fair for me to sleep while everybody is working."

"Today was hard, but tomorrow will be even harder. I need you rested."

He watched Pa step off his horse, hand the reins to Naldo, and head to the cook fire. The tall man's heels dragged in the dirt, and his shoulders drooped. Will slid off Blackie and turned him in with the other horses. An uneasiness swept over him. *Pa doesn't look so good. He needs to sleep, too.* He watched Pa drink his coffee. *But he won't.*

Smokey rode up with Two Feathers. "Rope me a fresh one, Naldo," he said. He looked at the Indian. "Old Pony can't keep up. Get another mount."

Naldo walked up, leading a horse. "Charlie says everyone stays with the herd tonight," he said.

Smokey watched Two Feathers walk among the horses. "The cattle are so thirsty, they won't bed down. We'll push 'em on. It's gonna be a hard night."

Will sucked in his breath as Two Feathers reached out to grab Buck's mane and called out to Smokey in Comanche.

Buck tossed his head and backed away.

Will yelled, broke into a run, and flung himself at Two Feathers. Buck sidestepped. The two boys landed in a heap on the ground, fists swinging. Naldo slipped a rope on Buck and dragged him away. Smokey grabbed Two Feathers and pulled the boys apart.

"That's enough!" Pa ran up and yanked Will away.

"Boy!" Smokey shook Two Feathers. "I told you that horse was Will's. You can't ride him."

Charlie Goodnight rode up. "What's going on here?"

"Will jumped the Indian when he tried to take Buck," Pa barked. "We're gonna have to do something about this, Charlie. I'm not gonna stand for him trying to get Buck much longer."

Several of the drovers gathered around. Hard eyes glared at the Indian. Defiant eyes glared back.

"Now, wait a minute, Dan." Smokey pointed to Will. "Your boy started this fight. I know Two Feathers wants Buck, but I've told him he can't have the buckskin. He's enough Comanche to be crazy about horses and to want the best horse he can find. I'll see what I can do to find one in the remuda he'll take to."

"Naldo, bring the grullo. I think he'll be able to ride him." The trail boss fastened hard eyes on Two Feathers.

"Mr. Goodnight, he can't have that horse," Will exploded. "That's your horse!"

"Will." Goodnight turned a stern face to the boy. "If you want him to leave Buck alone, he'll need a good horse. Comanche are horsemen. He needs a horse he can respect. The grullo is strong, tough, and fast."

"But he's not a drover. He's a prisoner. Why does he have a horse at all?"

Goodnight took a deep breath and blew it out. He put his hands on Will's shoulders. "I know you're worried about Buck. We won't let him get your horse. When we get to Fort Sumner, we'll turn the boy over to the army. They'll take him to the reservation in the Nations."

Naldo roped the grullo and led him to Mr. Goodnight. Smokey spoke in Comanche as he pointed to the gray horse. Two Feathers looked from the grullo to Mr. Goodnight then back to the old man, a puzzled expression on his face.

The Indian walked around the gray. He ran his hands down the strong legs and over the deep chest. When he finally looked at Mr. Goodnight, his head jerked in a quick nod.

Will looked at the drovers.

"Curtis?" he asked as the stocky cowboy mounted to ride back to the herd.

"Sorry, Will-boy. The boss can do what he wants with his own horse."

Anger exploded from Will's pounding heart and pumped through his body. He felt it quiver in his veins. *That Indian may get the grullo, but he'll never get Buck.*

Will turned his back on the men, went to the chuck wagon, and crawled underneath. *I don't like it. I just . . . don't . . . like . . . it.* He put his hand in his pocket and rubbed the green ribbon. Will watched Smokey walk with Two Feathers to the cook fire.

"Boy, come out here," the old scout called to Will, then turned to Cookie. "Feed these *fightin' men* and see they stay with the wagon. It's going to be a rough night."

Will flopped over on his back and studied the bottom of the wagon. *If he thinks he's gonna get Buck, he'll get a good taste of my fist.* He heaved a sigh and kicked the wagon wheel. *Ride in the wagon. Who ever heard of a drover ridin' in the wagon?*

"Two Feathers, you're worn plum out. You better stay in camp with Cookie," Smokey said.

An angry shout of Comanche burst from the boy. Smokey responded with a stern voice and headed for the herd.

Cookie dipped each boy a plate of beef and beans. "Will, get out from under the wagon and get your supper before I give it to someone else."

The growl in Will's stomach was louder than his anger, and he crawled out from under the wagon.

"Eat this and roll up in your blankets in the chuck wagon," Cookie told Will and Two Feathers. "The way them cattle are bawlin', it'll be hard going for the wagon to keep up."

Will lay in his blanket and glared at Two Feathers.

I know that Indian will go after Buck. I'm gonna watch him all night. If he gets up, I'll smash his nose again.

HORSEHEAD CROSSING

"Will, wake up," said Cookie, shaking the boy's shoulder.

Will sat up. "Is it morning?" He looked for Two Feathers and saw him standing in the pale predawn light.

Will stomped into his boots, rolled his blankets, and jumped down from the wagon. There was no fire. No morning coffee. No hot biscuits.

Pa handed him some jerky to chew on. Naldo had Buck, the grullo, and several other horses saddled and ready to go. Pa boosted Will onto the tall buckskin and handed him a full canteen.

"Remember, go easy on the water. We don't have much left."

Will didn't look at Pa. His eyes narrow, he watched as Two Feathers sprang onto the grullo and rode after Smokey.

"You hear me, boy?" Pa shook Will's leg.

"Yes, sir, I hear you." He looked at Pa. "Why'd Mr. Goodnight give the grullo to that Comanche? He's got his own horse to ride."

"I don't know. That's Charlie's business. Take a good look at Two Feathers's horse. Maybe that'll help you understand. Just keep your mind on those cattle and stay away from him. We have enough to worry about just getting the herd across these alkali flats. The thirstier these cattle get, the more dangerous they'll be."

The cool desert night faded as the sun appeared. By midmorning, the heat and dust once again put cows and cowboys in misery. The drovers took turns riding into the noon camp, staying just long enough to grab jerky and a cold, hard biscuit, fill their canteens, change their tired mounts, and head back to the herd.

Late in the afternoon, Will stopped Buck to let him rest.

Pa rode up. "You all right, son?"

"Listen. Do you hear that?"

The cattle's dry squeak of the day before had become a low moan. They stared from sunken eyes. Their ribs stood out like bars on a cage, and swollen tongues hung from their mouths.

"I don't think they're going to make it." Will took a small sip from his canteen. He slipped off Buck. Wetting his bandana, he wiped Buck's nostrils and mouth.

"Most of them will make it. Longhorns are tough." Pa reached down, grabbed Will's outstretched hands, and swung him onto the tall buckskin.

"Does Buck look thin to you?" He rubbed his friend's neck and stroked the long black mane, his fingers catching in tangles.

"Maybe a little. He'll be all right when we get to water."

Will and Pa rode up and down the long line of slow-moving cattle. The drovers' yells became hoarse croaks. To keep the cattle moving, coiled lariats slapped bony rumps. The weakest animals stopped moving and were left behind.

Will heard Curtis yelling and watched him driving a cow away from her downed calf. He raced over to the cowboy, jumped out of the saddle, and ran to the calf on the ground.

"What are you doing? It needs its momma."

"It's dying."

Will looked up at the hard, set face.

"It can't go anymore." The man's voice bit at Will. "She has to go on, or she'll die, too. Get out of here."

"No, you can't do that." Panic seized him in its vise-like grip. His breath came in quick gulps. He stooped over and tried to lift the calf. "Help me. We can get him up." It flopped limply on the ground with its tongue hanging from the side of its mouth. The eyes glazed.

Curtis's already red face turned purple. He flung himself off his horse, grabbed Will, and threw him on Buck. He gave the horse a sharp slap on the rump. "Get, Will."

Startled, Buck raced up the line of cattle. Will looked for Pa and found him up ahead.

"Pa, Curtis is leaving a calf behind. Its momma wants to go back, but he won't let her." Anger etched deep furrows across his forehead.

A shot sounded.

"Pa?"

"It has to be done, Will. You leave Curtis alone. Sometimes being a drover means you have to make hard choices you don't want to make."

Pa rode after a slow-moving bunch and swung his lariat to get them going.

As Will rode along the parched river of cattle, the sight of the downed calf with its tongue flopped in the dirt haunted him. Other calves lay stretched out on the desert floor. He hoped he never had to make that kind of decision. That sick to-bacco feeling hit his stomach. He didn't want to see any more.

The sun neared its western bed, and the sky changed from white-hot to fiery-red and orange. The night meal came and went, and still they pushed the cattle forward.

Will trailed behind his father as they once again rode point.

"Pa," he called and spurred Buck to catch up. "I'm glad Ma's not with us. She wouldn't like this awful place." Will lifted his canteen to his dry, alkali-coated lips and drank the last bitter drop. "I'm out of water. I'm going to the wagon to get some more."

Pa's red-rimmed eyes blinked several times as he looked at Will. He swallowed hard and cleared his throat. "I know, son." He took a deep breath. "You shouldn't be out yet. We filled up just a few hours ago. I warned you about drinking it too fast."

"I didn't drink all of it. I wet my bandana and squeezed it in Buck's mouth."

"Oh son, Buck will make it. He's strong. Tell Cookie to give you a little more, and don't give it to Buck."

Will rode toward the chuck wagon. He passed Two Feathers and Smokey riding swing. The Indian lifted his canteen to his lips and shook it. He showed it to Smokey and rode into camp behind Will. Cookie carefully poured a little of the precious water into each boy's canteen.

"That's all, boys. Don't come back wantin' more 'cause there won't be any. By daylight, this barrel will be empty. It's the last one. I can't even make coffee."

Will and Two Feathers rode back to the herd, too tired to think about their differences. The moon cast its eerie, white glow over the skeletal cattle. The dust hung over the herd like a veil.

Will looked around him at the drovers and cattle as they plodded through the night. "I don't like this place."

"Hard land. All hard land."

Surprised that Two Feathers had spoken to him, he glanced in his direction. Even in the moonlight, Will could see the weariness. He snuck another look. Dirt streaked the brown face. The feathers braided in his hair hung ragged and worn. *I wonder if I look as bad as he does,* he thought. *This is hard on him, too. I wonder where his family is.*

Mr. Goodnight rode up to the boys as they reached the herd. "What are you boys doing here? Turn your horses over to Naldo and catch up with the wagon. Tomorrow will be a rough day."

That night, the boys made no protest.

The next morning, Charlie rode up to Dan. "Take over point, Dan," he said. "Smokey and I are going on ahead to the Pecos. I need to see how far away we are. We'll take the canteens and fill them. We should be back by early afternoon."

The day had not progressed far when Will watched Two Feathers slip off Old Pony and walk. Every rib on the old horse stuck out like slats on a worn-out barrel. His head hung nearly to the ground. The smallest rock made him stumble. Worry clouded Two Feathers's face. Will looked away and patted Buck's neck.

The sun climbed higher. Cattle staggered after Ol' Blue. More dropped behind and were left.

I wonder if we will have any left to start a new ranch. Will chewed his bottom lip. He eagerly looked to the west for the boss to return. When a cheer started at the head of the herd and passed from drover to drover down the line, he smiled. *Water.*

Will's parched throat welcomed the wet relief, even though it was bitter with alkali.

Goodnight told the men to hold the cattle at Castle Gap, about twelve miles from Horsehead Crossing. "The crossing is narrow. With steep banks. Lots of quicksand. Take the stronger cattle first. When they smell water, they're going to stampede. I want four riders in front to hold them back. Dan, keep the weaker half in the canyon. Bring them on in after five or six hours. Maybe we won't lose the whole herd. Naldo, bring the remuda with the first bunch. You, too, Cookie. Keep Will with the wagon."

"We'll hold 'em." Pa looked at Will. "Leave Buck with the remuda and get in the wagon."

"I don't want to stay with Cookie. I'm a drover. I need to be with the herd."

"It's too dangerous. Stay with Cookie!"

"Pa, I don't want to ride in the wagon."

Pa's eyes narrowed. He stepped toward Will, yanked him up, and tossed him on the wagon seat. "You stay put!"

Will watched Pa ride toward the herd. He scrubbed his face with his sleeve, pulled his hat low over his eyes, and slumped on the seat. His breath came in quick, short gasps.

Cookie climbed onto the seat beside Will. "Dan is right, Will. Things are going to get awful bad before they get all those cattle to the river."

Will said nothing.

With the end of their ordeal in sight, the drovers pushed the herd with renewed vigor. At Castle Gap, they divided the cattle. Goodnight and his men pushed the stronger cattle out of the canyon. Naldo and another drover bunched the remuda on the far side of the herd. Will held onto the wagon seat as Cookie bounced the chuck wagon over rocks and clumps of brush slightly ahead of the cattle. He searched for any sign of the Pecos.

·144·

"Cookie, will there be green grass and trees like on the Colorado or the Concho?"

"I don't think so. This is desert country."

In a few hours, the animals caught the scent of water and broke into a wild stampede. Will stood in the seat. The point men stayed with the lead runners as the herd swarmed past the wagon.

"Sit down," Cookie yelled as he fought to hold the mules back. They smelled water and tried to break loose from Cookie's control.

Will sat and braced himself, holding on tight as the chuck wagon bounced and rocked over the desert floor. The pounding of his heart matched the pounding of hooves. Will looked for Buck but could see nothing through the thick dust. "Cookie, where's Naldo with the remuda?"

Cookie yelled at the mules. His strong, thick arms fought the reins that jerked and bucked in his hands. He didn't even look at Will.

The herd hit the Pecos at a run. The cattle in the rear pushed the first ones that reached the river all the way across before they had time to drink. The point men had to turn them back to the water.

Again, Will stood in the wagon seat and watched as the force of the cattle pushing from behind caused the herd to spread out. Some of the cattle ran off the bluffs into the quicksand, where they floundered, lunging in the thick, sucking mud and sand. Drovers uncoiled their lariats and pulled cattle to safety. The ones beyond reach sank beneath the quicksand.

As Cookie and Will moved north along the Pecos looking for a campsite, Will worried about the calves and their mommas coming with the rest of the herd. *How will they ever get across?*

Cookie didn't give him much time to worry about calves. They found a camping spot with a narrow trail down to the river, upstream from the herd. Will jumped off the wagon and Cookie told him to explore and see if he could find a place deep enough to fill buckets. "Go slow, Will. Watch for quicksand. I don't want to have to rope you out of the mud like a steer." Cookie took the mules to the crossing to drink.

Will made his way through the thorny catclaw and lotebush to the embankment over the river. As far as he could see in both directions, the Pecos River twisted and turned like a snake, weaving its way through the desert. He picked up the bucket, then slipped and skidded down the path to the river's edge. A small sandy beach, white with alkali, provided easy access to the river. Will flopped on his belly. Even the bitter water didn't stop him from soaking his hot face and head in the wet coolness. It stung his eyes and his cracked lips. He drank it, anyway.

He sat by the river, pulled off his boots, and soaked his hot feet in the water. *I hope New Mexico isn't like this. Cows can't live here.* He closed his eyes and thought of the ranch back home, the grass waving in the wind, and the bright sunflowers his mother had loved so much.

The hot sun soon dried his feet. He pulled his boots back on. As he dipped the bucket in the water, he noticed an unshod horse track in the mud where the water eddied around a rock. *When did Two Feathers change from riding the grullo to Old Pony?* he wondered. *What's he doing this far upstream?* He filled the bucket, then headed back up the steep path. As he walked, he looked for the remuda with the grullo and Buck, but couldn't see them anywhere.

"Will, this bucket is only half full." Cookie frowned at Will and poured the water in the coffee pot.

"I started with it full. That path is steep."

"Okay, let's both go. I'll have some of the men fill the barrels. These two buckets should get us through dinner." When they got back, Cookie and Will worked to set up camp and start the evening meal. For shade, they strung a tarp from the back of the wagon to poles Cookie drove in the ground. Will gathered wood and buffalo chips for the fire.

Curtis came riding up, leading Buck. "Naldo said he's had some water and for you to let him drink slowly. Just a little at a time."

"Thanks, Curtis." Will ran to the big stallion. "Hey, Buck." He hugged him. The horse flipped his hat off and snuffled his hair. Will picked it up. "Aw, Buck. My hat's a mess already. Don't make it worse." He poured some of the water from a bucket into a wash pan and let the horse drink. Buck pricked up his ears and looked back across the desert.

"What is it?" Will followed the horse's gaze to a billowing cloud of dust and heard the distant sound of bawling cattle.

"Cookie, the rest of the herd is coming."

"I hear 'em," Cookie said.

"I'm gonna go watch 'em come in." Will stepped up on the wagon wheel, grabbed a handful of mane, and slid onto Buck's bare back. He tapped him hard with his heels. They took off at a gallop.

"Will, come back here!" Cookie yelled. "Those cattle will be crazed for want of water. Stay away from 'em!"

Will didn't answer. He rode toward the coming herd in the distance. Hoofbeats sounded behind him. He looked back over his shoulder. Two Feathers came up from the river at a lope, riding the grullo. Will leaned forward and wrapped the mane tight in his hands. "Go, Buck. Two Feathers and that gray horse can't beat us." They took off at a full gallop.

Will heard pounding hooves behind him and turned to see Two Feathers leaning forward in the saddle. Will kicked Buck hard. Both horses raced past the remuda, which was coming up from the river and spreading out over the desert to graze. A bend in the twisted river snaked between the racing boys and the thirst-crazed, stampeding herd.

Naldo yelled to stay away from the cattle, but both boys raced on toward the bend, Buck in the lead. The wrangler spurred his mount and took off after them.

Wild screams erupted from the river. A band of Comanche swarmed up out of the bend and swooped down on the remuda.

The noise made Will turn in time to see a Comanche in yellow and black war paint coming at a gallop. He watched in disbelief as the Indian rode straight for Two Feathers. At a full gallop, he nocked an arrow in his bow and shot. It barely missed Two Feathers, but Naldo fell from his horse with the arrow in his shoulder. Two Feathers turned the grullo aside and headed toward the river. He rode the gray horse off the high embankment.

With the sound of a hissing snake, two ropes settled around Buck's neck. An Indian galloped on each side, holding the ropes tight. The Comanche fled, taking a dozen horses back toward the bend in the treacherous Pecos.

And in their midst raced Buck—and Will.

CAPTIVE

"Pa!" Will screamed.

Twisting as far as he could without falling off, he looked for riders coming to his rescue. He saw only Comanche in fierce war paint.

"Pa, help me!" Will screamed again. *No. No. No,* shrieked in his head. "NOOOOO!" burst from his lips in a loud wail that trailed after him like the howl of a banshee.

The air around him seemed too thick to breathe. He gulped at it in short, quick gasps. He jerked Buck's mane, trying to turn him. The Indians' horses pulled Buck, making him gallop faster. He tossed his head, but the ropes squeezed tight.

The riders shortened their ropes and moved in close on either side of Buck. They raced across the flat desert. *Pa, Pa,* Will tried to yell, but the words caught in his throat. One of the Comanche men leaned close and slapped him hard on the back of the head, knocking Will onto Buck's neck. He had to grab more mane to keep from falling.

In his fight against the ropes, Buck stumbled. Fear for Buck made Will ease his weight forward and kick Buck's flanks.

The horse regained his footing, easily keeping pace with the Indians' horses.

"Buck! Oh, Buck." Tears whipped from Will's eyes. With his heart racing and his legs shaking, he struggled to stay on the galloping horse.

The big buckskin's ears turned back toward his friend.

Will looked at the Indians riding on either side. On his right, black paint covered the man's face from forehead to nose and red paint from nose to chin. Red and black paint swirled around his arms and chest. The man on his left had one side of his face striped up and down in brown and the other side striped side to side in black. Their long black hair streamed behind them in the wind. Even their horses were painted.

Will turned again to look behind him.

No Pa.

No Rory.

No Curtis.

No Mr. Goodnight.

Only more Indians driving horses.

A sob burst from him, and the wind sucked the tears from his eyes. Will leaned forward and buried his face in Buck's mane. The Comanche on his left laughed.

As the hours passed, pain racked his whole body and drove out everything but mindless terror. His worst nightmare had come to life.

Darkness fell. Occasionally, they slowed the horses to a walk to let them rest and catch their breath. Will eased himself up off Buck's sweat-soaked back and shifted his position. The constant rubbing against his wet jeans set the skin of his legs on fire.

But they never stopped. They'd kick the horses into a gallop again and race on. Will worried that Buck, already tired from the drive to Horsehead Crossing, would fall, but the big buckskin stayed on his feet, weaving and dodging between the desert shrubs.

Sometime during the night, they followed a steep path down to the river. They rode along the water's edge for a while, then crossed and climbed up to the desert floor again. The horses and some of the warriors managed to drink a little. Will started to dismount when Buck dipped his head to the water. But a stocky Indian, with half his face and body painted yellow and the other half black, barked at him and pushed him back on Buck. His throat burned. He longed for a taste of the water, but the man with yellow paint only laughed at him.

Daylight slowly eased across the sky. Will hoped they would stop for food and water, but they rode on. The sun burned his back and the right side of his face, so he knew they were heading northwest. As he rode, he looked around for something he could use as a landmark, but everything looked the same. No trees, just clumps of grass, scrub brush, and cacti. The sun climbed overhead.

Finally, they stopped at a clear running creek, flowing through mesquite trees. Will slid off. His legs collapsed, and he fell to the ground. The Indians laughed. They led Buck to the water with the other horses. Will rubbed the numbness from his legs. They were still shaky and he wobbled some, but he made it to the creek, buried his face, and drank the cool, sweet water.

He sat still, relieved not to be riding. *How far is it back to the herd? When will Pa come get me? How will he ever find me?* whirled through his mind. The throbbing in his head spread to the back of his eyes and down the back of his neck. Hunger pains stabbed him. He hoped they would build a fire and cook some food. They didn't.

The man with yellow and black paint tied Buck to a tree, then walked around the horse, admiring him and running his hands over him. When he touched Buck, Will stiffened. A growl slipped from his lips.

Buck sidestepped and rolled his eyes to see the Indian. He laid his ears flat against his head. The Indian spoke to the others and grinned. When he passed behind him, Buck kicked. The Indian jumped out of the way. The others laughed.

"Leave him alone, he's mine!" Will ran to Buck and stood at his head. The horse snuffled his hair. Will reached up and wrapped his arms around the horse's neck. Both watched the painted Indian. Will narrowed his eyes in defiance. "Don't let him see you're afraid," he whispered to Buck. Again, Buck laid his ears flat and snorted. Will wrapped his hands tight in the mane.

The Indian walked toward Will and backhanded him. Will staggered from the blow but stayed on his feet. The Indian spoke in a stern voice, then pointed to a tree. Will knew the man wanted him to sit by the tree, but he shook his head.

"I won't leave Buck!"

The Indian grabbed Will's arm and slung him across the clearing. He landed in a heap at the base of the tree. He cried out as his head smacked the trunk. Blood trickled down his face. The pounding in his head seemed to shake the ground. Buck's screams sliced into his headache like a knife. Will sat straight up. The sudden movement turned everything black. He dropped his head between his knees to keep from passing out.

Buck's long tail lashed across his hunched body with the sting of a whip.

Will lifted his head. The stallion stood in front of him, the rope he had been tied with hanging from his neck. Buck lunged at the painted men. Yellow Paint caught a glancing blow on his shoulder from a slashing hoof. He fell and barely rolled away before the ironshod hooves crashed to the ground.

Will pulled himself up and leaned against the rough trunk of the tree. He wiped his forehead, and his hand came away covered with blood. A moment's confusion left him immobile until Buck lunged with teeth bared at one of the men coming at him. A rope hissed from behind and settled around Buck's neck, pulling tight. Then a second. Then a third.

"Stop!" Will screamed and scrambled around the thrashing hooves. Will knew, if Buck didn't calm down, they would choke him until he fell to the ground. Buck stood quivering with his head hung low and his tongue out. Will jerked on the taut ropes and looked from one Indian to another while stroking and talking to Buck to keep him calm.

The man with red and black paint let some slack in his rope and spoke to the others. They loosened theirs.

The stallion sucked in air and stepped between Will and the men. His ears lay flat against his head. He pawed the ground and snorted.

Will moved in front of Buck and raised his hands. The proud head settled between Will's arms. They stood together, each wary but comforting the other.

Yellow Paint walked toward them, swinging a small loop in his riata of braided leather strips in his hand. When Will put his hand out, palm up, to stop him, an angry burst of Comanche exploded from the man, and he raised the riata and expanded the loop. Buck again stepped in front of Will. Red Man pulled Yellow Paint away and motioned for Will to control the horse. The two men argued, each pointing at Will and Buck. Will decided Red Man won the argument when Yellow Paint did not toss the riata around Buck's neck but walked away and threw himself on the ground near the fire.

Red Man led Buck and Will to the creek. Dipping his bandana in the water, Will held it to his bleeding head. Watching from the fire, Yellow Paint laughed.

Tears threatened to slip down Will's face. *No,* he thought. *I won't cry again.* He took a deep breath. *I won't ever let them see me cry.*

Will sat on the bank of the creek, bathing his head, until his captors motioned him to mount up. He stepped toward Buck, but Yellow Paint shook his head, grabbed him, and set him behind Red Man.

Will kicked at the man and slid off the back of the horse. He ran toward Buck, but two of the Comanche threw him, belly down, across the horse in front of the Indian.

"No! Buck!" He kicked and pummeled the Indian's legs.

The warrior whacked him hard on the head and back until he stopped yelling. Will grabbed the horse's mane and hung on. The Indian kicked his horse into a lope.

The Comanche, with ropes keeping Buck under control, drove him and the other horses up the creek at a fast trot. The cold water splashed and soaked Will. His ribs and belly throbbed with every step the horse took. He lifted his head to see Buck, but could not find his horse.

Time crawled into what seemed like forever. Finally, the Indian stopped long enough to lift Will into a sitting position. They rode on, hour after hour. Despair settled over him like a hot, smothering cloak.

Night came, and still they didn't make camp. Will finally passed out from exhaustion and hunger.

He opened his eyes to daylight and found himself on the ground. Every muscle hurt. He stifled a groan as he got to his feet. When his vision cleared, he spotted the horses watering at a small stream. Buck stood tied between two trees. Will hobbled to him.

"Your muzzle is wet. That's good. You got some water." Will scratched under the matted mane. "You're a mess. When we get back, I'll work on your mane and tail." Buck lowered his head. Will hugged his friend. "Oh Buck, I should have listened to Pa and Cookie." His throat tightened, and he couldn't speak. He sucked in a lungful of air and slowly let it out. His tension eased a bit. "Look what I've done to us. I'm sorry, Buck. I'm so sorry."

Tears threatened again as he heard footsteps behind him. He forced the tears back.

Yellow Paint dragged him away from Buck. He barked at him in Comanche.

"Buck is mine! You can't have him." Will clenched his fists. His body tensed with anger.

The Indian grinned, pointing to Buck, then to himself. He laughed at Will and walked off.

Will collapsed against a tree, dropped his head on his knees, and rocked back and forth. He could hear the Indians talking as they walked among the horses. *Where am I? How far did we come? It's been two nights and two days. How will Pa ever find me?*

Desperation filled his heart. *We are alone.*

He didn't know how long he sat under that tree, but slowly, a small flame of anger built in his heart and grew until it replaced the anguish.

I have to be tough, like Buck. I can be strong.

He lifted his head and looked around. *I don't know which way to go, but somehow, we will leave here.*

For a while, the Indians ignored Will. They laughed and talked to each other as they admired the horses. One short, stocky Indian caught a hard kick from Buck and yelped in surprise and pain.

Will smirked. "Good job, Buck," he whispered. *I'm so proud of you. You're strong. I know we'll make it.* A plan slowly formed in his mind. *I'll do what they say and not cause trouble. Then maybe they won't watch me so close. Buck needs rest and lots of grass so he'll be ready when Pa comes.* He felt better and went to the creek for a drink.

Once more they rode all day and through the night. Hunger grew into a living demon in Will's belly. They finally stopped the next morning. His legs buckled when the Indian dropped him from the horse. He staggered to his feet.

Barren land spread before him. Few trees grew there, only more scrub brush and clumps of grass. Off to the west, he could see the outline of distant mountains. *Too far.* He hadn't counted on this. *We're too far. Pa can't find me here.* He no longer felt the hunger pains. He no longer felt thirst. He no longer felt anything except a dizziness in his head that said *I'm lost.*

With his hand in his pocket clutching the green ribbon, he rolled over on his side and passed out.

COMANCHE SLAVE

A sharp pain in his ribs jolted Will awake. He looked around, trying to figure out where he was. Pain again. Yellow Paint shoved him with his foot. The Indian spoke and motioned him to follow. Will's heart raced as he struggled to his feet. *Why does he want me?* Half of the orange ball showed over the western horizon. *I slept all day.* The inside of his legs burned from three days of riding bareback. Raw skin stuck to his pants where the blood oozed. His muscles were stiff and sore. His stomach rumbled.

Yellow Paint pointed to the fire where a pot of meat boiled. Will stood still. The Indian went to the pot, picked up a stick, stabbed a piece of meat, and gave it to him. With another stick, he took a piece for himself and ate. Will lifted the meat to his nose and sniffed. It didn't smell bad. He ate. The Indian motioned for him to get more. Will ate his fill.

Yellow Paint handed him a large water pouch and carried one himself. He motioned to Will. Uncertain what the man wanted, he followed the Indian down a path through the bunchgrass and greasewood. Will spotted horses not too far away. He looked for Buck but didn't see him. *Where's Buck? What have they done to him? If he's hurt, I'll kill that devil.*

They came to a pool in a narrow creek with low, steep banks. The water ran past where the horses grazed. Yellow Paint stepped off the bank onto some rocks. Will followed. They filled their pouches. The Indian showed him how to tie the top so the water wouldn't spill.

Back at camp, Yellow Paint pointed to a pile of skins under the low-hanging branches of an old mesquite tree near the fire and indicated for him to sleep. Will crawled onto the skins and lay down. They were musty and smelled of smoke.

What if Pa never finds me? That thought drove sleep away, and he lay for what seemed a long time. He thought of all Pa had done for him. *My new hat—that must have cost a lot of money. His hat is old and about worn out, but he got me a new one. I didn't take care of it like he told me. He showed me how to be a good drover. I've done everything wrong. I didn't stay in camp. I stayed mad at him all the time.* He choked on a sob. *If he comes, I'll do what he tells me, no matter what it is.*

He remembered the boy who had been taken by the Comanche last summer from around Fredericksburg. *He's been lost a whole year.* Will bolted upright. *What if Pa doesn't want to come get me? I've been so ugly about leaving Ma behind, maybe he doesn't want me anymore.* Face buried in his arms, he wept, stifling his sobs to hide them.

A coyote howled. Will's eyes popped open. He didn't remember falling asleep. He lifted his head and looked for the Indians. Red coals dimly showed the sleeping men. He lay still for a while, trying to decide what to do. No sounds drifted through the night. A coal shifted on the fire and blazed up. *Where am I? Oh, Pa. Where are you?*

Not moving and barely breathing, he listened. One of the Indians snored. Will sat up and crawled out from under the branches of the tree. Nothing happened. He stood. Nothing happened. He walked a short way from the camp.

I can't run now. I don't know where Buck is. Carefully, he retraced his steps and lay back down. He looked at the sleeping men. No one moved. His stomach ached for food, and his throat burned for water, but his feet wouldn't let him go close to the Comanche. Exhaustion from three days on the back of a horse dragged him down. He closed his eyes and slept.

The crisp call of a nighthawk woke him. He stood in a fog of total blackness. A tiny light blinked in the distance. As he moved through the darkness, he could neither see nor feel anything. Their cabin back at the ranch formed within the light. He looked in the window. His mother sat at the kitchen table, brushing her hair. She picked up a green ribbon. Running it through her fingers, she showed it to him, then tied it in her hair.

"Be brave, my cowboy." Her words filled his whole body.

He wondered how he could hear them because her lips never moved.

He woke—really this time—and stirred on his bed and stretched. Hot, stinging pain seared his chafed legs as his pants rubbed against his oozing skin. The soft moonlight flickered through the lacy mesquite branches as he waited for the pain to pass. He slipped his hand in his pocket and pulled out the green ribbon. Running it through his fingers like Ma had done, he smoothed out the wrinkles. *Pa said Ma would always be with us, that we weren't leaving her behind. I can be strong. Pa will come.* Somehow, he felt comforted.

The men worked him at camp chores off and on all the next day. They watched him but didn't bother about where he went as long as they could see him. As he collected fuel for the fire, either sticks or buffalo chips, he spotted the horses but didn't see Buck. A couple of times, he left to get water from the creek and stayed briefly out of sight of camp.

One of the warriors, after killing a small deer with his bow, was furious when Will couldn't skin it and cut up the meat. He yelled at him and put his hands on both sides of Will's head and waggled it back and forth, then rolled his eyes. Will decided the man thought he was stupid. The warrior showed him how to skin it, then gave him a knife and taught him how to cut it up. When Will finished, he put the meat in the pot, and the man took the knife, to Will's despair. He'd hoped the Indian had forgotten it.

The afternoon of the second day in camp, Will went to get water from the creek. The herd of horses grazed on a grass that grew in tall bunches, like a shrub. He spotted Buck, staked on the far side of the herd. He looked to be in good shape, and Will almost cried out in his relief at seeing the horse. He watched him for a while.

On his way back, he saw Yellow Paint coming. The Indian grabbed Will's arm and dragged him back. His angry words left no doubt in Will's mind that he had been gone too long. Yellow Paint spoke to one of the men with black paint covering his face and nodded toward Will. The Indian grinned at Will and pointed a stout stick at him. Yellow Paint walked away in the direction of the horses.

The rest of the afternoon, Will watched for Yellow Paint's return. He heard Buck call, heard the other horses snort and whinny. *What are you doing to him? Don't hurt him.* Black Head, as Will called him, grew increasingly frustrated with Will's inattention and his constant stopping to look toward the horses. The blows from his stick fell more and more across the boy's back and legs as evening approached.

Will was adding wood to the fire but stood when he saw Yellow Paint storm into camp. Rage etched hard lines on the Indian's face. Will spotted dried blood on his shoulder and a large hoof-shaped bruise on his leg. Will dropped the wood on the fire and launched himself on the Indian's back. He wrapped his legs around the man's waist and his arms around his throat.

"What did you do to Buck?" Will screamed. He pummeled the Indian's head and shoulders.

The warrior reached back and grabbed Will to swing him over his head. Will grabbed handfuls of long hair and hung on. He kicked and screamed at Yellow Paint.

"If you hurt Buck, I'll kill you!"

Yellow Paint jerked Will free, threw him to the ground, stomped him, and drew his knife. Will watched the knife as it rose and started down.

A hand grabbed the wrist and wrenched the knife loose before it reached his throat. Red Man pulled Yellow Paint away, but not before the angry Indian kicked Will in the head. They left him lying in a heap.

Pain reached deep into his fogged brain. Rolling over set his muscles on fire. He choked back a moan. His eyes opened. The sun had set. Only faint colors remained in the western sky. He sat up. Trying to decide how badly he was hurt, he sat still. A slow, deep breath woke the ache in his side. Even though it hurt, he didn't think any ribs were broken.

He stood and watched the men around the campfire. The guard from the horse herd came into camp. They were eating, laughing, and talking. No one noticed him. He walked to the creek, wet his bandana, and wiped his face.

I don't care what they do to me. I have to see about Buck. He followed the creek bed until he saw the horse herd and climbed up the bank. He didn't see any guard. A rope held

Buck's head tight to a mesquite tree so he couldn't lower it to graze. Sand and dirt dulled his coat, and burrs tangled his tail and mane. His knees showed dried blood, and rope burns circled his neck. Rage and hate swelled within Will until he thought he would burst. It settled low in his heart, like the glowing, burning pile of hot coals in a blacksmith's forge. He slipped over the bank, took a quick look around, and raced across the open space.

"Buck," he whispered and reached up to untie him. The horse lowered his head. Will's arms went around his neck. "Oh, Buck, what have they done to you?" He led Buck down to the creek, and the horse drank. Will pulled his head up. "Not too fast, Buck. Take it easy." He examined him carefully. "You don't seem to be hurt too bad." He let him drink again. "We can't go yet. I don't know where we are. I'll have to figure something out."

He let Buck have one last drink and a few bites of the bunchgrass, then took him back to the mesquite tree and tied him up. "I'm sorry, Buck. I don't want you to follow me, or them to know I've been here. I'll come back for you."

Will slipped back down to his spot on the bank near camp. He had just dipped his bandana and wiped his face when Yellow Paint walked up. The Indian motioned for him to return to camp. Will's knees weakened with relief that the man had not discovered his absence, and he stumbled when he climbed up the creek bank.

Yellow Paint pointed to the pot simmering on the fire. Will took a hunk of meat and went to the mesquite tree. After eating, he pulled his skins to the other side of the tree, away from camp. Not wanting to even see the Indians, he pulled his bed as far as he could. He stopped when one of the men walked over and frowned at him. Tree branches and darkness hid all of the camp but the glow from the fire.

Lying on his back, he watched the sliver of moon rise through the lacy, narrow leaves of the mesquite. Footsteps approached. Will tried to keep his breathing even, as though he were asleep. The footsteps stopped. Yellow Paint spoke, but Will didn't move. The footsteps retreated back toward the fire.

Somehow, I'll get away. Pa is looking for me. I know he is. This creek flows east. If I follow it, maybe it will take me to the Pecos.

Will lay on his skins and tried to figure out a way to get one of the water pouches without Yellow Paint or the others knowing. Ideas whirled through his head. The stars winked as clouds passed through the night sky. A slight wind picked up sand and skittered it across the desert. He faded into sleep.

A strong hand clamped over Will's mouth. Will's eyes flew open, and he fought the weight pressing him to the ground.

"Quiet," a voice whispered.

Still he fought.

"Will," the voice said in a hoarse whisper.

Will froze. *English!*

THE RACE

Two Feathers slowly lifted his hand from Will's mouth and rolled off him. Will sat up. The Indian put his finger to his lips and motioned for Will to follow.

"What . . . ?" Will whispered.

Two Feathers shook his head and covered Will's mouth. "We go," he whispered. He worried that all the noise Will made following him would wake Yellow Hawk. They crouched low and crawled away from camp, hindered by the dim starlight.

Two Feathers stopped often to listen. The sounds of the night teased his ears. He ignored the ordinary scurrying of the night hunters and listened for any sound not natural to the desert.

Slowly, they moved farther away from camp. Will stepped on a stick. The snap sounded as loud as a gunshot in the still night. Both boys froze. Two Feathers strained to hear any sound. Silence. He grabbed Will's arm and shook it. "No," he whispered.

Hugging the shadows and avoiding a patch of prickly pear cactus, the two boys circled wide, away from the creek and farther from the camp.

"Where's Pa?" Will whispered when they stopped. "How did you find me? How did you know where I was?"

"Smokey brings Dan," Two Feathers said.

Will sank to the ground. "I knew Pa would come."

Two Feathers started off again then stopped when Will pulled his arm.

"Buck," Will whispered.

"Dunnia," Two Feathers answered.

Will looked puzzled. Two Feathers grinned and motioned him to follow. Will shook his head. "I have to get Buck."

"Dunnia. Buck."

Two Feathers started off again, relieved that Will followed quietly this time. A short run brought them upstream and downwind from where the horses grazed. Easing into the creek bed, they worked their way downstream.

When they reached the horses, they stopped and looked over the edge of the bank. The dark shapes of the grazing animals dotted the desert. Two Feathers grabbed Will's arm and pulled him down when he raised his head too high. "Wait. Warriors watch the herd."

They studied each bush and shrub, waiting for movement. Will raised his head again. "Buck," he whispered and pointed to the horse snubbed up tight to the mesquite tree.

Two Feathers waited. He looked up at the clouds covering the moon. Only a few stars winked through the cloud cover. *Where is he? If Barks Like Coyote guards the herd, we will get away easy.*

Still, Two Feathers waited.

Will stretched his foot. His boot slipped on a rock. It tumbled down the bank, landing in the creek with a soft splash. Both boys flattened in the dirt below the rim of the creek bank.

Two Feathers put his hand on Will's back to hold him still. He could feel the other boy's muscles quiver under his hand.

Two Feathers waited.

A shadow moved. A form separated itself from a dark cluster of bushes across the clearing from Buck and headed toward camp. Two Feathers and Will watched it disappear into the darkness. They eased themselves over the bank and ran in a crouch to the mesquite tree. Will put his hand on the horse's muzzle to quiet him. He untied Buck. They moved cautiously away from the herd.

At a safe distance, Two Feathers boosted Will onto Buck's back. He saw the grimace when Will's legs gripped the horse and looked quickly away. "Grab on," Will said and stuck out his hand.

Two Feathers looked up at him in surprise, then took a firm grip on the outstretched hand. With a nimble leap and some furious scrambling, he managed to sit astride the tall horse behind Will. Two Feathers grabbed Will around the waist to keep from sliding off when Buck snorted, pranced, and kicked his hind legs. A pat on the neck and a word from Will calmed the nervous horse.

They headed southeast, away from the creek, at a quiet walk. Every sound made Two Feathers jump, and he turned often to look behind him. He felt Will's body twitch and jerk at every night sound. Two Feathers finally let go of Will's waist because the other boy kept twisting from one side to the other to look around him and down their back trail. Shadows of bushes and trees pursued them, and fear blew in the wind.

An hour of riding at a mile-eating lope brought them to a shallow, narrow river. Two Feathers motioned for Will to head Buck into the riverbed. The Indian hoped it flowed with enough water to cover their trail. As they neared a cluster of stubby trees, he pointed to the grullo staked in their midst. He slipped off Buck and mounted.

"Wait, where are we going? Do you know where we are?" Will said.

The welts and lumps Two Feathers had felt on the thin body he had gripped on their ride explained the fear in Will's voice. He pointed. "River goes to the rising sun and to Pecos." He rode up the bank and out onto the desert floor, then headed east at a full gallop. Will rode beside him.

They traveled hard and fast into the night for as long as the tired horses could take the pace. Two Feathers slowed the grullo and walked him to the river. Will rode up beside him. Both boys and horses drank. Two Feathers led the horses away from the water.

He handed Buck's reins to Will. "Rest." He swung his arm to the east. "We still have a long way to go." Will collapsed on the muddy bank and closed his eyes. Two Feathers caught the reins and wrapped them around Will's hand. The tired buckskin stood with his head hung low. For a long time, Two Feathers watched their back trail. Satisfied no one followed, he tied the grullo's reins to his wrist. Trusting the horse would wake him if disturbed, he went to sleep.

A sharp tug on his wrist woke Two Feathers. The grullo jerked his head, trying to reach the water. The sun burned hot, sitting in the haze a good ways above the horizon. Two Feathers stood and walked the grullo to the riverbank. They both drank.

Suddenly, the horse lifted his head. His ears stood straight up. He turned toward their back trail. Two Feathers climbed up the embankment and searched the desert. Movement of a dust cloud in the not-too-far distance made him tense every muscle, and cold sweat slicked his palms. He ran back to the river, slid down the embankment, and gave Will a hard shake.

"Yellow Hawk!" His voice cracked at the hated name, and he leaped astride the grullo. Wading his horse into the water, he looked back at Will, who stood frozen beside Buck, his eyes wide.

The grullo took a few steps, but Will didn't follow. Two Feathers stopped and waved for Will to come on. "Ride!" he yelled.

Anger tore at Two Feathers as Will remained frozen on the riverbank. Only his head moved, first looking toward him and then down their back trail.

Realization hit. *The horse is too tall, he can't get on the dunnia.* He rode back toward Will.

"He is too small for that big horse," he snapped in a burst of Comanche.

Astonished, he watched as Will slapped Buck's leg and the dunnia dropped to his knees. A handful of mane, a quick scramble, and they headed toward him.

"Come on," Two Feathers said. "Stay on the rocks. Do not go in the mud."

They walked their horses in the river as quickly as Two Feathers's caution would allow.

"We need to hurry," Will complained, repeatedly twisting around to watch behind them.

"We leave no tracks on the desert for Yellow Hawk to follow. No dust for him to see." He put his fingers to his lips for Will to be quiet.

The soft splash of hooves or the light click as they struck rocks seemed to echo within the banks of the riverbed.

They followed the river's twists and turns through the morning. The minutes inched by. The scrubby trees that grew along the river blocked any breath of air from the desert floor. The dry heat grew, and sweat soaked horses and riders. Each time Two Feathers turned to look behind him, he expected to see Yellow Hawk coming in the distance.

A tangled cluster of driftwood blocked their way. The horses lunged up the embankment and back down on the other side of the clogged waterway. Two Feathers passed places where it would have been easy to leave the water and make faster time on the desert floor, but the river hid their tracks. He knew it wouldn't fool Yellow Hawk, but it might delay him for a while.

A gravel bar spread out on one side of the river. Two Feathers finally walked the grullo out of the water and onto the rocks. He followed the gravel bar until it blended into the sandy ground of the desert, giving way to sacaton grass and creosote bushes.

He looked at Will. Dark circles surrounded the boy's eyes. Sunken cheeks gave him a hollow look. His fists, tangled in the mane, showed white knuckles.

He tires. He will not last much longer. Yellow Hawk will kill us both if he catches us. Fear sickened Two Feathers's stomach. He knew Running Wolf would not be able to stop Yellow Hawk this time.

The sun beat down straight overhead. The twisted turns of the river led them east toward the Pecos. The water grew shallower and soon disappeared, leaving thick mud. The smell of decayed vegetation mixed with the sharp odor of the gray-green creosote bushes.

Two Feathers pulled away from the river and farther onto the desert floor. The alkali dust that rose from the horse's hooves burned his eyes and tasted bitter on his lips. He looked back to see a cloud of dust coming fast behind them.

"Yellow Hawk!" he cried and kicked the grullo.

·169·

He heard Will's yelp and the pounding of Buck's hooves beside him. They raced across the desert, weaving between the clumps of creosote bushes.

An arrow whistled between them and took Two Feathers's fear with it. Anger, from deep in his heart, welled up and replaced the fear. Yellow Hawk had killed his father and tried to kill him. Two Feathers twisted on the grullo and looked back to see his uncle nock another arrow. As he kicked the grullo for more speed, he raised his fist, and a Comanche war cry burst from his lips.

A second arrow flew past. The hot whoosh of its death song skimmed past the grullo's hip and his own leg. His horse surged forward. They passed the arrow where it stuck quivering in the ground.

Above the pounding of his heart and the pounding of the horse's hooves, he heard Will scream, "Run, Buck!" The dunnia's long legs stretched out for more speed and flew over the ground, leaving Two Feathers and the grullo behind.

From the southeast, a second dust cloud moved toward them. A deep boom sounded. Two Feathers looked back to see a warrior tumble off the back of his horse and bounce as he hit the ground.

A rifle popped. The boom sounded again. Another Comanche hit the ground. Relief swept over him like a cool breeze as Two Feathers watched Yellow Hawk and his warriors veer off to the north.

Smokey! Two Feathers slowed the grullo, but Will and Buck did not stop. He watched Smokey gallop toward him. Dan turned his horse to intercept Will.

Riding up to Two Feathers, Smokey slipped his big Sharps .50 rifle into its boot and stepped down from his horse. Two Feathers jumped off the grullo and into Smokey's bear hug.

"John!" Smokey let go and stepped back to look at him. "I knew you didn't run off with the Comanche stealing the remuda. I knew you didn't!"

Two Feathers backed away from Smokey. Relief at seeing the old man stretched a wide grin across his alkali-caked face.

"I followed Will and the dunnia. I leave you good trail?"

"Yes, you did. It will take some explaining, but I think the others will understand. They think you ran off with the Comanche."

"Yellow Hawk!" Two Feathers spat on the ground. "My enemy tried to take the dunnia. But I got him back. He will not have him. And I took his captive. He has nothing."

TURMOIL

The terrifying war cry that burst from Two Feathers chilled Will to the bone, and he knew the Indian had not come to rescue him but to get Buck. He kicked Buck and drove him to even greater speed. Two Feathers and the grullo fell behind.

Will heard the deep boom of a big gun. Every terrifying story he had heard about the fierce Comanche exploded in his head. The wind whipped Buck's sweat from the horse's body and soaked Will's clothes. His legs cramped in agony while gripping Buck's sides. But he stuck to the slippery, wet horse like a sticktight seed and bent low over the buckskin's neck, the two moving as one. To fall meant death.

Dodging clumps of sacaton grass and leaping over creosote bushes, they raced across the desert. The wind roared in his ears, blocking all other sounds. His fear of capture coursed through him like a raging fire.

Will wrapped his hands tighter in the long mane. He felt Buck falter. *No! Buck! Don't give out now.* The words screamed in his head, but he knew the horse could not maintain his pace much longer. He glanced over his shoulder. A rider cut across the desert, coming closer. A new wave of panic swept over him. His thoughts spun like a whirlpool, sinking his head into Buck's flying mane and darkness.

"Will? Wake up," Pa said. "I'm here, son."

Will's eyes focused. "Pa!"

Pa cut Will's hands loose from Buck's mane. Will slid from the horse, and Pa eased him to the ground. Grabbing his canteen from his saddle horn, Pa wet his bandana and wiped Will's face. Each cooling stroke slowed Will's racing heart as it cleaned away the dirt and sandy grit.

Pa scooped Will into his arms. Will's grip locked around Pa's neck.

"Pa. Oh, Pa."

Their tears soothed the terror in their hearts.

"Dan, we need to get off this desert and find cover," Smokey said quietly as he and Two Feathers rode up. "I don't know if those Comanche will come hunting us again."

Pa put Will in front of him on his horse. Will called to Buck. With hooves dragging in the dust, he followed.

Smokey scouted for a secluded place to hide. A gravel bar alongside the river under an overhanging bluff provided cover. Pa, Will, and Two Feathers drank from the river while Smokey watched their back trail for signs of pursuit.

Two Feathers walked Buck and the grullo until their breathing slowed. He took them to drink and then tied them so they could nibble on the leaves and whatever grass they could find.

Will watched Two Feathers with the horses. Memories rolled through his mind—*the cemetery . . . the baby calf . . .*

the fishing hole. He didn't save me. He thinks he has Buck. Anger surged through him like the roiling Colorado.

"Get away from my horse!" he shouted and ran to Buck. "That's all you've ever wanted." His voice rose to a higher pitch. "You've tried and tried to get him. You got him away from Yellow Paint so you could have him for yourself." He shoved Two Feathers away from Buck.

"Will," Pa said. "Stop!"

"He just wants Buck." Hysteria pushed Will's voice to a brittle squeak. His fists clenched. His face flushed hot. "Yellow Paint took me because he wanted Buck, too."

"Two Feathers tracked you for days. He left a trail for Smokey and me to follow. If he only wanted Buck, he would have stolen him and left you there. Think about it."

Pa took Will and led him away. They sat under the overhang in the shade. "We'll talk about it later. You boys and your horses need to rest before we can travel."

Will's eyes followed Two Feathers. Pa's words swirled in his head, mixing with his fear for Buck and his confusion about Two Feathers. *He did find me first.* He took off his hat and wiped the sweat from his forehead. *But he always wanted Buck.* He closed his eyes and rested his head in his arms. *I don't know what to think.* His stomach rolled over, and he ran for the river. He retched, but his empty stomach had nothing to give up. He heaved until the spasms finally passed. When he looked up, Pa was by his side, handing him his wet bandana.

"Come on, son. You need to rest."

Will followed him back to the cutout and stretched out. Pa went to care for Buck. Will looked for Two Feathers. They stared at each other. Two Feathers turned his back to Will and put his arms around the grullo's neck.

Will's head hurt. Exhaustion made it hard to think. *Every-where we go, someone tries to get Buck. Nobody bothered us at home.* Watching Two Feathers brush the grullo, he thought about what Pa had said. He thought about how Two Feathers got him out of the Comanche camp. *He did come back for me.* He snuck a quick glance at Two Feathers standing by the grullo at the river. He thought about how much he cared for the grullo.

Three days later, a tired and dusty foursome rode into camp on the Pecos. They had followed the Delaware River east before turning south and had caught up with the herd about halfway to Pope's Crossing. Excitement at their arrival spread through the camp and to the men guarding the cattle. Smiling faces surrounded them as they dismounted.

"Welcome back, Will," Rory said, grinning ear to ear. "You all right, boy?"

Will didn't answer.

No one greeted Two Feathers.

"Thank goodness you found them." Charlie shook Dan's hand.

"I see you caught that Comanche again, Smokey," said Russ. "You still gonna keep him in camp after he led those Comanche right to us?"

"We don't know what Two Feathers did," said the trail boss before Smokey could reply. "We'll hear their story at supper. You men get back to work."

Russ finished his coffee and set the cup by the coffee pot. "I don't know why they brought that Comanche back."

"The way he took off after the horses, I'm sure he knew them Indians was comin'." Rory pitched his cup on the ground beside the others.

Hank walked up, leading three horses.

"You don't know that's true. Don't make up your mind till you hear what they have to say."

"I don't trust that Indian," Russ mumbled.

Will watched the three men ride off. Tangled thoughts whirled in his head. *Pa said Two Feathers helped find me, and Rory said he helped the Comanche.* He picked up Buck's reins. *I don't know. He's tried and tried to steal Buck. Why does he stay here?*

He walked Buck to the chuck wagon.

"I'll take Buck to Naldo and turn him in with the remuda," said Pa, taking the reins from Will.

Will backed up to Buck and stood under his neck. He reached up. The horse lowered his head between the boy's raised arms. "No. What if they come back? I need Buck close, in case I need to get away."

"Buck needs to graze, Will. He's thin, like you. You know you're hungry. So is Buck. Mr. Goodnight has three men guarding the remuda. Smokey is going to circle the herd to watch for trouble. Let me take him. It's the best thing. I'll put extra oats in his feed bag tonight."

Will looked up at Buck. He buried his face in Buck's long mane, then nodded. "After he's grazed for a while, bring him back, okay?"

Goodnight drank the last sip of his coffee and put his cup on a rock near the fire. "Will, remember, I said you could keep him in camp at night. I'll take him. Dan, you tend to Will." He reached for the reins and led Buck toward the remuda.

Will followed Pa to the campfire. Cookie handed each of them a cup of hot coffee.

"Cookie, heat some water," said Pa. "You got somethin' to doctor Will's cuts and bruises? He pretty well rode the hide off his legs."

While Cookie's stew simmered on the fire, he warmed buckets of water. Will sniffed the stew. "I'm hungry, Pa. Can we eat first?"

"It's not ready. You go with your pa." Cookie dipped more water from a barrel strapped to the side of the wagon and poured it into an iron pot. He set it near the fire.

"Cookie," Will's voice trembled, "I'm sorry I rode off when you told me to come back. This wouldn't have happened if I had done what you said. If I had paid more attention to you."

"I know you're sorry, Will-boy." He pulled his big red bandana from his pocket, blew his nose, and wiped his eyes.

Two Feathers walked up and handed Cookie some dried condalia root. "Weeping Woman used this to wash wounds. Boil it in the water. It will help take away the pain."

Will watched as Cookie poured the ground root from a small leather pouch into the water. *Why did he give that to Cookie? What does he want?*

Pa and Will went behind the chuck wagon. Will stripped off his shirt and handed it to Cookie. He cried out in pain when Pa worked his pants from his raw legs. While the old man washed the clothes, Pa washed Will's wounds with the tea.

"What did they do to you?" Pa asked, his voice low and husky, his face grim, his touch gentle.

Will gasped from the sting when the warm water washed over his raw skin.

When it was over, Will wrapped in a blanket and sat next to Pa near the fire. Cookie filled their plates with stew. Will watched as Two Feathers sat across the fire and devoured his supper. *What's going on with him? What does he want here? Why doesn't he go home?*

The men rode into camp as each shift changed. Pa told them about Will's rescue by Two Feathers and their long ride back to the herd.

Curtis sat beside Will. "Are you all right, Will-boy?" He put a rough, callused hand on Will's shoulder. "Did they treat you okay?"

Will looked away from Curtis and pulled the blanket tight.

"I don't think the boys are ready to talk about what they've been through. Let's leave 'em a little room," Goodnight said.

"Now maybe we can get these cows up the trail," said Jake. "Without you, these ornery critters didn't want to go no-where."

Tony grinned at Will.

"That's right," Curtis said. "These animals been draggin' their feet and doing everything they can to keep from making progress."

Charlie laughed. "Oh, it's the cattle that's dragging, is it? What about all the long faces and the eyes that watched for dust clouds coming from the west? Let's get back to work."

Will looked at the men but said nothing. He watched them as if he sat a long way off, his mind still a confused fog. Their words seemed to bounce through his fear and weariness, like echoes in a cave.

"Pa." Will blinked several times, trying to focus his eyes. "I'm tired."

Wrapping the blanket tighter around him, he stood and walked to the wagon tongue where Cookie had spread his clothes to dry. Digging in the pocket of his damp jeans, he pulled out the ragged green ribbon and folded it in his hand.

Pa spread their bedrolls out from the fire, but close enough for a dim light to reach them.

The quilt from home that Pa folded inside Will's bedroll felt cool after Cookie's hot, scratchy wool blanket. Trying to find a spot that didn't hurt, he rolled over on his stomach. He traced his fingers over the stitching.

"Pa," he whispered. "Ma came to see me in the Comanche camp." He held his breath, waiting to see what Pa would say.

Silence.

A tree frog croaked his loud call.

Pa was silent for several minutes, then cleared his throat. "I told you before we left home she would always be with us."

"You were right." Will closed his eyes.

STAMPEDE

The herd moved north, up the west side of the Pecos River. Will stayed in the wagon for three days. On the third day, Smokey and Two Feathers rode into camp in time for supper.

Will dropped an armload of wood near the fire. His shoulders drooped when he watched them ride in, pick up their plates, and take them to Cookie. Smokey filled their cups with coffee. They sat together on the ground and ate their supper. Will held his plate out for Cookie to fill.

"I thought Two Feathers went home. I haven't seen him for three days. Why is he back here?"

"He went with Smokey to scout the trail to Pope's Crossing." He handed Will his plate. "Did you know Two Feathers's real name is John Randall? He and his pa had a ranch together. Like you and your pa. Smokey knew his father. He's been talking to Two Feathers about him, helping him remember." Cookie filled Will's cup. "Go easy on him. He may not be what you think he is."

Will sat by himself and ate his supper. His wayward eyes kept sneaking peeks at Two Feathers.

The next morning, Will convinced Pa the wounds on his legs had healed enough for him to ride. He followed Tony and Jake to the herd and worked the flank position with them. About midday, Pa rode up to get him for the noon meal.

"You all right?" Pa asked.

"Sure." Will squirmed in the saddle, trying to take the pressure off his still sore legs.

Pa grinned. "You did good this morning, but I think you need to ride in the wagon this afternoon."

Will didn't argue.

As the last of the drovers finished their meal, Cookie started packing up to head for night camp.

"Will," he called, "climb in the chuck wagon and get me another sack of beans. They need to soak before I cook 'em."

Will took a few minutes to work the bag loose from under the heavy flour sacks. As he started to climb out of the wagon, he heard Two Feathers and Smokey walk up. He stayed out of sight.

"What are they going to do with me?" Two Feathers asked Smokey. "I heard them say they would give me to the soldiers."

"I heard that, too." Smokey leaned against the wagon wheel.

Will felt the wagon move. He sat still.

"What will the soldiers do with me?"

"I reckon they'll take you to the reservation in the Nations."

"Why can I not stay with you?"

"Because I don't have a home. I move around all the time."

For a while, Will heard nothing, then the wagon shook as Smokey pushed himself off the wagon wheel.

"John, you need to decide what you want to be. Do you want to be John and make a place for yourself in the white man's world or be Two Feathers and live on a reservation and be Comanche?"

"I do not know what I am."

"There are good things about both, John. You need to think about it."

Will ducked as they walked around the front of the wagon and dropped their plates in the wash bucket. He sat there, stunned. *But he is a Comanche. He wants to steal Buck. That's what he has always wanted.*

"Will," Cookie yelled. "Where's them beans?"

He scrambled out of the wagon and gave the bag to Cookie. The rest of the afternoon he barely spoke, and Cookie kept asking him if he felt all right.

All the next day, Will watched Two Feathers. Wherever Two Feathers rode, he worked nearby. Grudgingly, he admired his horsemanship. He could ride bareback as well as most men rode with a saddle. In the morning, he rode his old pony, and at noon camp, he changed to the grullo. Before he turned the old horse in with the remuda, he brushed him with care and checked his hooves.

The afternoon wore on, hot and dry. Will saw Two Feathers stop the grullo and slide off. He picked up a front hoof.

"What's wrong?" Will asked as he pulled up beside the gray horse.

"Little stone," Two Feathers said, holding up a pebble he'd pulled from under the horseshoe. He grabbed the strap he had tied around the girth of the horse, mounted, and rode after a wandering steer.

Will watched him ride off. *He takes good care of his horse.* It suddenly occurred to him that Two Feathers no longer seemed focused on Buck. *What's on his mind? Maybe he's happy with the grullo.* He rubbed Buck's neck. "You think he's gonna leave you alone? I sure hope so."

Curtis rode up. "What's on your mind, Will-boy? You're just sittin' there. The cattle are wandering everywhere. It don't take a lot of smarts to be a drover, but you do have to keep your mind on the job."

Will tapped Buck with his heels and kept up with the cowboy. "What's gonna happen to Two Feathers?"

Surprise spread all over Curtis's face as he looked at Will. "Goodnight is gonna hand him over to the soldiers at Fort Sumner. Since when do you care?"

Will didn't answer. He urged Buck after a wayward calf.

Early the next afternoon, Smokey, on a lathered horse, caught up to Goodnight, Dan, and Will at point. "We got buffs comin'. They're a ways behind us, but movin' fast."

Pa grabbed Buck's reins and pulled him tight against his horse. Alarmed at Pa's intensity, Will looked straight at him. Pa's dark tan had paled.

"Go to Cookie and stay with him. Tie Buck tight to the wagon. He's never seen buffalo. He's going to spook." He let go of the reins.

Will turned Buck, and Pa slapped him hard on the rump. Will grabbed the saddle horn to keep from falling off when Buck jumped into a gallop.

He rode toward the chuck wagon. *Buffalo! I'm not going to miss this.* He turned off before he got there and headed back toward the drag riders, excited and completely forgetting his new resolution to mind Pa.

The drovers popped cattle with their lariats to speed them up. Pa, Goodnight, and several others fired their revolvers into the air to start the cattle running. Goodnight seemed to be everywhere as he rode up and down the stretched-out herd, yelling at men and animals. Naldo drove the remuda at a gallop away from the cattle.

Will heard a low rumble, like a continuous roll of thunder. The ground shook. The nervous cattle quickened their pace. Will saw fear in their eyes.

The buffalo appeared out of a moving cloud of dust. As one massive body, the herd broke into a crazed stampede. The buffalo overtook the cattle, and the stampeding animals surged ahead as one huge avalanche of sharp, pointed horns and huge, wooly heads.

Buck spun around and galloped away from the strange-smelling animals.

"No, Buck!" Will yelled. "I'm not missin' this."

For the first time in his life, Buck fought against Will. Hauling hard on the reins, Will finally pulled him to a stop. He stroked, patted, talked, and they took off again after the stampeding hoard. Will's heart raced, and he pushed Buck to keep pace with the mixed herd. Grit filled his eyes, but he refused to look away from the terrifying but incredible sight.

The cattle panicked. The stampede rushed across the desert like the torrent of a wild river of hairy, bobbing heads. The drovers pulled away from the melee of horns and hooves. They raced to keep up with the panic-driven cattle, working the ones on the outside away from the buffalo. The terrified cattle in their midst did not faze the huge, hairy beasts. They ran over everything in their path. Calves. Cows. Steers. Nothing stopped them. Dust rose in thick, yellow clouds. The rumble became a deafening roar.

Will rode Buck on the outskirts of the stampede. He leaned far forward and shouted, "Go, Buck. Run!"

The big stallion twitched back his ears, stretched out his long neck, and bellied out. From his deep chest and brave heart, he once again gave the boy all he had.

Will barely noticed the pain in his chafed legs. He pulled his hat tight onto his head. *What a sight!* Dust rose in thick, choking clouds. The roar of hooves thundered in his ears, blocking all other sounds. Will's nose filled with the stench from the black, wooly beasts.

Will spotted Two Feathers, an arrow nocked in his bow and a full quiver strapped on his back, racing Old Pony next to a large bull. The Indian leaned toward the buffalo and shot his arrow into the shaggy beast. With accuracy and speed, Two Feathers shot two more. The buffalo bellowed, swung his massive head, and ripped Old Pony with his horns. The horse pulled away from the running beast and tumbled head over heels, throwing Two Feathers to the ground. He jumped to his feet and ran to his fallen horse. Will spotted a tight bunch of cattle and buffalo racing straight for the fallen Indian.

"Two Feathers!" Will screamed but could not be heard over the deafening noise. He turned Buck hard, and they galloped toward the downed Indian. He looked back at the stampeding animals and urged Buck to even more speed.

"Two Feathers!" Will yelled as loud as he could. He shifted his weight to the outside stirrup, the pain in his legs screaming, grabbed the saddle horn with one hand, and leaned across Buck.

Two Feathers grabbed the outstretched hand and swung himself up behind Will. Buck turned away from the thundering mass of sharp horns and hooves and carried both boys to safety.

The thunder of the buffalo herd rolled past, diminishing to a low rumble as the shaggy beasts disappeared in the distance. The ground stopped its terrible shaking. Scattered cattle were everywhere—some standing and some smashed and trampled on the ground.

Through the dust hanging in the air, the boys stared at the carnage around them. They rode Buck to Old Pony. Only a trampled carcass remained.

Two Feathers closed his eyes. "My father gave him to me when I was very small. Now I have nothing." He hung his head. A low moan seeped from him.

Will stood silently beside him, his heart felt like a boulder in his chest. It felt like the day they buried Ma.

Two Feathers lifted his head and looked off in the distance. "I am Comanche. I will not speak his name again." He turned and walked off.

With his pocketknife, Will cut a long lock of hair from the mane. He dug in his pocket and pulled out the green ribbon, tied it around the hair, and pushed it deep to the bottom of his pocket.

Leading Buck, he caught up with Two Feathers.

"Ride with me. We need to find Pa or Smokey."

The boys scrambled onto Buck and followed the trail of the stampede. Neither spoke. At an outcropping of rock, Will dismounted and sat down in the shade. Two Feathers slid off Buck's rump. Ignoring Will, he walked away from the trampled trail.

"Why did you come after me?" Will called. "Was it to get Buck?"

"No. I have a warrior's horse. Gray Wolf. You have dunnia."

"Why did you save me?"

Will stood and caught up with Two Feathers. He searched the stoic face.

Two Feathers sat and leaned against the rocks in the shade. Will dropped beside him, sitting on his heels. He studied the sun-tanned face and searched the gray eyes, trying to find an answer to his confusion.

"Does it matter?" Two Feathers asked.

"Yes. I don't understand what you want."

"Yellow Hawk killed my father. He beat me. Yellow Hawk took you from your father. He beat you. Yellow Hawk is my enemy. Yellow Hawk is your enemy. The enemy of my enemy is my friend."

Will collapsed against the rocks and dropped his head to his knees. The distant sounds of the drovers rounding up the remnants of the herd came to him on the hot, dusty breeze. He looked at Two Feathers.

"You don't want to take Buck?"

"Who would not want a warrior's horse like the dunnia?" Two Feathers grinned. "Gray Wolf is mine. Buck is yours."

Will stood. He felt as though a plug had been pulled from the bottom of his feet. All his fear for Buck drained out. For the first time in many weeks, he smiled.

Two Feathers boosted Will onto the tall buckskin. Will stretched out his hand and pulled Two Feathers up behind him. As they rode to find Pa and Smokey, Will's mind moved from his old worries about Buck to new worries.

How will we find a ranch? What will the soldiers do with Two Feathers?

FORT SUMNER

Will and Two Feathers collected scattered cattle and pushed them up the trail as they searched for Pa or Smokey.

Russ and Hank rode out of a draw, pushing about a dozen bawling cows and calves.

"You boys all right?" Russ called.

Will waved at them, nodded, and hollered, "You seen Pa or Smokey?"

"Ain't seen your pa. Smokey's up ahead, scoutin' for a place to hold what's left of the herd."

Buck's head turned at the sound of bawling from a bunch of steers in a shallow gully about a hundred yards off to the left. They skirted a trampled patch of cactus and rode toward the sound. Two Feathers slipped off Buck's rump and dropped into the gully. Driving their bunch, Will met him, pushing the wayward cattle out to where the gully flattened onto the desert.

They met up with Goodnight where he and some of the drovers held the herd on a flat away from the steep banks of the Pecos. The welcome sound of Ol' Blue's bell called many of the scattered cattle back into the herd.

"Charlie," Smokey said as he rode up, "I got a spot to hold the cattle upriver. The banks ain't too steep. There's pretty good grazin'." He looked at Will and Two Feathers. "John, where's your horse?"

Two Feathers turned away and did not answer.

"The buffalo got him," Will said.

Smokey studied Two Feathers's stoic face. "I'm sorry about that. You two go get the grullo."

They found Naldo, and Gray Wolf came to Two Feathers's call.

"I need to find Pa," Will said. "I need to talk to him about something."

Two Feathers stroked the gray horse's neck.

Will waited for his reply, but he got only forlorn silence. "I'll see you at supper."

He rode south along the river and spotted Pa riding toward him.

"Why didn't you go to Cookie, like I told you? Russ told me he saw you and Two Feathers on Buck. What happened?"

"Old Pony is dead. Buffalo killed him. Buck and I picked up Two Feathers. We took him to Naldo. He's on the grullo." Will hoped this news would take Pa's mind off his not going to Cookie.

"That's too bad. How's he taking it?"

"He won't talk about it."

"You leave him be. Comanche don't speak of their dead."

Will and Pa looked at each other. For once, Ma seemed to stand with them and not between them.

Pa smiled. "Time cures a lot of things."

In silence, they turned down a shallow draw and found a group of cattle grazing on bunchgrass. They started them toward the herd and followed the draw until it ended in a tangle of brush. There, they found about fifty head. They pushed them back down the draw and, catching up with the first group, drove them back to the herd. Occasionally, the sad sound of a shot rang out when drovers found an animal too badly injured to continue.

By afternoon of the second day, the herd stretched along the banks of the Pecos. Will was helping Cookie in camp and brought an armload of wood to the fire. Charlie and Pa came into camp from counting the herd.

"I consider us lucky," Charlie said. "It looks like we only lost about a hundred head."

"That's about what I figured," Pa agreed as Will filled his cup with coffee.

"We start for Bosque Grande in the morning." Charlie turned to Naldo. "How many horses did we lose?"

"None, señor. We ran the horses away from the búfalo."

"That's good. We can't stand to lose any horses."

Through the rest of the hot afternoon, riders fanned out over the countryside and brought in a few more head. The fiery-red orb sinking in the western sky welcomed the tired, dusty men plodding into camp.

Will and Pa brushed their horses down and turned them in with the remuda. They walked down to the Pecos, where they splashed water over their dusty heads and faces, washed their hands all the way to their elbows, and dried off with their bandanas. The shade of a rocky overhang gave them relief from the hot sun. They stretched out to rest.

Will draped his wet bandana across his forehead and cupped his hands behind his head. The red clouds fading to deep pink reminded him of the sunsets Ma had loved so much back home. That seemed like a long time ago.

"Pa, Charlie said we would head for the Bosque Grande tomorrow. How much farther are we going? You said we'd have a ranch in New Mexico. Where are we going to find it?"

Pa lifted his wet bandana off his face. "I've been thinkin' about that. Before we left Texas, Charlie told me about a place called Puerto de Luna. It means 'gateway to the moon.' Honey Allen told him how the land around there had plenty of grass and water. It's about halfway between Fort Sumner and Fort Union and not too far from Santa Fe. I was thinkin' we'd look around there and see what we could find."

"Any grass and water would beat what we've seen so far. I don't much like not having a home," Will said.

"Come and get it, boys, before I throw it out!" hollered Cookie.

Pa and Will climbed up the embankment. Their growling stomachs answered Cookie's call.

"I don't think Ma would like it here."

Pa stopped, looked at Will, and smoothed a stray lock of damp hair off his forehead. "Ma would be happy anywhere we were. The place wouldn't matter to her. But we'll look for a ranch you think she would have liked."

Will smiled.

Green. Beautiful green. Will stood with his hand resting on his horse's neck while Buck tore mouthful after mouthful of the tender grass. He closed his eyes and filled his lungs with air that held no dust. He held his breath. The clean, fresh air seemed to course through his body, chasing away the last of the alkali dust. When he let the breath go, some of the fear, tension, and worry gushed out with it. He opened his eyes and looked around.

If cattle could smile, there would be huge grins on all their faces. Every cow's head bowed low to the ground. The gentle sound of cattle ripping grass mixed with the soft clatter of leaves in the tall cottonwoods. Squirrels scolded and ran from limb to limb in the green canopy spread over the Pecos.

Will wiped his mouth after scooping up a handful of sweet, cool water. He flopped over on his back and stretched out on the green grass. "It don't seem like this is the same river. I sure like it better up here than down in that desert." He picked up his head and looked at Buck. "You're not even listening."

Birds fluttered from tree branch to tree branch. Will spotted a bright flash of a bluebird here, a red-breasted robin there, the *rat-a-tat-tat* of a woodpecker, the bright jewel of a hummingbird that dipped and darted through the air. At last, they'd reached the Bosque Grande, a beautiful oasis in the New Mexico desert.

"Hey, Buck," Will called and rolled over on his stomach. Propping his head on his hands, he watched as the big horse lifted his head. Grass hung from his mouth. He flicked his ears at a pesky fly. "I think I could live here forever. This would make a great ranch."

Buck stepped forward and ripped another mouthful.

Will picked a long blade of grass and stuck it between his teeth. "But Pa says we can't stay here. We need to be farther north."

He slipped his hand in his pocket and fingered the ribbon tied around the lock of Old Pony's mane. "Ma would have loved this place. Doesn't make sense to me." He lay on his back again and watched through the swaying leaves as the clouds drifted a lazy trail across the pale-blue sky. "Sometimes I just can't figure Pa out."

The herd rested in the luxury of Bosque Grande and filled up on the now sweet water of the Pecos for several days, putting sleek muscle back on their once cagelike, skeletal bodies. Then, with renewed vigor and full bellies, the river of cattle once again flowed north. A four-day drive brought mid-September with its refreshing fall coolness. And Fort Sumner.

The drovers bedded the cattle on good graze a couple of miles from the fort. Cookie set up camp between there and the river. The early morning air held a refreshing nip as Will, the trail boss, and Pa saddled their horses.

"Will," said Charlie, "where's Two Feathers? I told Smokey I'd take him to the fort this morning."

Will didn't look at him. "I don't know where he is." He stepped into Pa's cupped hands, settled into the saddle, and rode on ahead of the men.

Pa and Goodnight caught up with Will.

"Where's Two Feathers?" Pa's tone had a bite to it, and Will looked at him.

"I haven't seen him this morning." He tried to hold a casual look to his face, but worry made it feel stiff and flat. *Where did he go? I hope he didn't run off.*

"We have to turn him over to the army. They'll take him to the reservation in the Nations."

"I haven't seen him, Pa." Will looked back and forth between Pa and Mr. Goodnight. "I haven't. I looked for him but couldn't find him anywhere."

They rode on into Fort Sumner. Will watched the Indians that stood in groups, both outside the fort and inside the compound. They didn't look like the Comanche that had taken him. These Indians' thin bodies held no strength. Their eyes held no fire, their expressions no life. Their hunger showed too clearly.

"Pa," said Will, his voice shaky, "who are these Indians, and what are they doing here?"

"The army is holding the Navajo and Mescalero Apache on the reservation near here at Bosque Redondo."

"What's the matter with them?"

"They're on the verge of starvation, and General Carleton needs the beef to feed them," Goodnight said.

"Two Feathers can't come here." His eyes moved from one gaunt, lifeless face to another. Panic pricked him from inside his belly. He searched the trail boss's face for some idea of his plans for Two Feathers. "Mr. Goodnight, don't bring him to this awful place."

Neither man answered him. Fear for Two Feathers joined the panic, and the pricks sharpened.

They turned in the final tally of steers to Mr. Roberts, the general contractor for buying cattle. He paid eight cents a pound on the hoof. The agent wanted the bigger steers and not the smaller ones nor the cows and calves.

A blue-uniformed soldier approached them. "Mr. Goodnight?"

"Yes?"

"General Carleton asks you to join him in his office and to bring the boy that was captured by the Comanche."

Will looked at Pa. "What does he want me for?"

Charlie laughed. "Don't worry, Will, you're not in trouble. General Carleton heard about you. He wants to ask you some questions. You can leave Buck tied here. We're just going a short way."

The Indians in front of the agent's office watched the horse. Some even walked over to get a closer look.

"No," Will said, keeping a tight grip on Buck's reins. "He goes where I go." Will led Buck as they followed the men.

At the general's office, Will tied Buck to the hitching post and followed Pa. He walked to the sergeant sitting at a desk just inside the door. "Sir, please keep an eye on my horse. I don't want anyone to get him."

"Sure, son." The sergeant grinned at Will. "No one will take him on my watch. He's a mighty fine animal."

General Carleton stood as they entered his office. With a warm smile, he shook hands with the men, then offered his hand to Will. "This must be the brave young man that made that daring escape from the Comanche."

Will's face flushed red. He shook the man's hand but didn't speak.

"Be seated, gentlemen." He looked at Will. "I need as much information as you can remember. There's a small band of Comanche raiding in this area and east of here. I've received word from the general at Fort Bascom on the Canadian River that these raids are particularly vicious. We need to know who these Indians are. Could you tell who the leader was?"

"His name is Yellow Hawk," Will answered, looking at the floor. That sick tobacco feeling hit his stomach.

General Carleton came around to the front of his desk and knelt in front of Will. He looked directly in his face.

"What did he look like?"

Will closed his eyes. He didn't answer. His head ached, and he felt dizzy. *I don't want to talk about it* kept repeating over and over in his mind.

"I know it's hard to think about that time, son, but the army needs your help. What can you tell me?"

"He was mean," Will answered. "His eyes were hard and real black. He never smiled. He wanted my horse. I think he didn't kill me because Buck was good when I was there."

"I'm sure he wanted your horse. The Comanche only want the best horses. What did he look like?" General Carleton repeated.

"He was painted yellow and black. One side of him was yellow. The other side was black."

Carleton stood and looked at Dan and Goodnight. "That's him, Yellow Hawk. Soldiers from Fort Bascom got a look at him, and they said the same thing." He turned back to Will. "Can you describe any of the others?"

"One had the top of his face black and the bottom painted white. He and Yellow Hawk talked a lot. He made me skin a deer and got mad when I didn't know how."

Pa put his hand on Will's shoulder. "I think that's enough, General. Will hasn't talked much about his capture. I don't want to push him too fast."

"I understand, Mr. Whitaker, but Will has information we desperately need. This is a brutal Indian. We must find him. The army wants him on the reservation in the Nations or in jail."

"I'm okay, Pa." Will straightened in his chair and looked General Carleton in the eye. Taking a deep breath, he said, "What else do you want to know?"

"Do you have any idea where they took you?"

"I know we went northwest. Back home, Pa taught me to use the North Star at night and the sun by day to know where I am. We rode for three days, almost without stopping. I was afraid for Buck. They didn't stop to let him eat or drink much. We came to a creek and followed it west for a while. Sometimes the creek had water in it, and sometimes it didn't. Finally, we camped at a place where there was a lot of water. The creek kind of pooled. We stayed there for three days. When I got away, I followed that creek east. That's where Pa and Smokey found me." Will stopped talking and rubbed his eyes, as though to scrub away the awful memories.

"General," said Pa, "Smokey told me the creek Will is talking about is the Delaware River. We followed it back to the Pecos and caught up with the herd below Pope's Crossing."

"Thank you, Will. You've been a big help. You're a very brave young man to have survived such an experience." The general turned to Dan and Goodnight. "Yellow Hawk is the one we're looking for. He's raiding through Eastern New Mexico Territory and escaping into the Llano Estacado. He knows that country, and our soldiers don't. It's amazing Will was able to get away. He's very lucky."

They left the general's office. The sergeant at the door grinned at Will. "There's your horse, son, all safe and sound. I only had to fight off half the Indians in New Mexico, but I saved him for you."

Will grinned at the soldier. "Thank you, sir."

Goodnight stayed behind to make the final arrangements for transferring the cattle to the pens behind the fort.

Pa and Will headed back to the herd. "Did we get enough money to buy us a ranch?"

"We'll register a quarter-section homestead. That's one hundred sixty acres. We don't have to buy that. And we'll free-graze the land around it, and yes, I think it will be enough to get a good start. I kept the better cows and calves and a couple of good bulls."

Pa stopped his horse, looped a leg around the saddle horn, and fanned himself with his hat. "Why didn't you tell the general that it was Two Feathers who rescued you?"

"What?" Will exclaimed. "The soldiers might have taken him away and put him on this terrible reservation. The Indians here have no life in them. It's as if they have no spirit. Besides, Two Feathers is going to live with us."

With a laugh, Will whipped off his hat and slapped Buck's hip. As they galloped back toward the herd, he swung it in a circle over his head with a wild "Yee-haw!"

Pa's startled horse jumped, nearly pitching him off. "Wait a minute!" Pa hollered. "Who said he was going to live with us?"

The next couple of days, the drovers sorted cattle and delivered them to the agent from Bosque Redondo. Will and Two Feathers worked alongside Pa, separating their cows, calves, and bulls from Goodnight's cattle.

On the second afternoon, Will and Two Feathers rode their horses down to the Pecos for a quick drink. Will splashed his face. As he wiped it dry with his bandana, he asked Two Feathers, "What are you going to do? Are you going with Smokey?"

Two Feathers held Gray Wolf's reins as the horse drank. "Smokey says I cannot go with him. He says he has no home for me. Goodnight says I must go to the reservation in Indian Territory." He dug his toe in the mud at the edge of the water. He did not look at Will. "I do not know."

Will's heart quickened. "Isn't your name John Randall?"

Two Feathers raised his eyes to meet Will's. "Yes," he said with a puzzled expression.

"I told Pa you could live with us." Will's words tumbled out in his excitement. "We need help on the ranch. If you wore clothes like me and said your name is John Randall, it would work."

"What did your father say?"

"He didn't say anything yet, but I know he'll say yes."

"That is what I thought about Smokey."

By the end of that day, the drovers had the cattle that had been sold to the army grazing behind the fort. Cookie bought fresh supplies and fixed a dinner of ham and potatoes with dried apple pie. Will stretched out on the ground a little ways from the men. Loosening his belt to relieve the pressure on his full stomach, he thought about Two Feathers. *I can't get Pa or Two Feathers to say yes. Maybe if we take Two Feath-*

ers to the fort and he sees how those Indians live he'll decide to stay with us. Maybe that will work. With a plan in mind, he wondered if he had enough room for one more piece of pie.

Mr. Goodnight poured himself another cup of coffee and called the men to come close around the fire. "Dan, Smokey, and I have been making plans," he told the men. "We made good money on this trip, and I think we can make more. In the spring, Russ is taking the cattle we have left on to Denver and selling them up there. I'll head back to Texas and bring another herd. Dan and Will are staying here to build their ranch."

Will watched as Two Feathers followed Smokey out toward the remuda. They stopped a little way from camp and talked for a while. Two Feathers looked upset. Will headed toward them but stopped when he saw Two Feathers turn and walk off.

"Will," Smokey called.

Will walked over. "What's Two Feathers going to do?"

"I don't know," Smokey answered. "I told him to stay here with you and Dan. Make a home for himself. But he wants to come with me. I don't know what he'll do."

"He can stay with us, Smokey. I'm sure it will be okay with Pa. We need help on our new ranch," Will said.

"Your pa and I have been talking about it. He said he'd think on it."

Will grinned. "Thanks, Smokey."

He took off to look for Pa.

JOHN RANDALL

Will found Pa sitting back from the campfire, talking to Mr. Goodnight, their long legs stretched out, hats tilted to the backs of their heads, leaning against the wagon tongue. He hung back, waiting for them to finish their conversation. He didn't want to interrupt if it was something serious.

Not interrupting just might help keep Pa in a good mood. Will made circles in the dirt with the toe of his boot and waited. He sat on his haunches and waited some more. Then stood and waited even longer. He walked in a circle, sneaking glances at Pa. *What are they talking about that could take so long?*

"Will," Pa called, "what are you doing?"

Taking a big breath, he walked over. "I need to talk to you. It's important."

"Is it about Two Feathers living with us? Charlie and I have been talking about that."

"He doesn't have any place to go or anyone to live with."

"He has family, Will. Smokey says he's been living with his mother's family for the past five years."

"He can't go back there. Yellow Hawk will kill him." He looked hard at Pa's face—every inch of it. His heart raced with the need to make Pa see the danger.

"What is it, Will?" Pa stood. "What's wrong?"

"If you send him back, Yellow Hawk will kill him."

Pa stared at him. "You really believe that, don't you?"

"No, Pa. I don't just believe it. I *know* it!"

A change came over Pa's face. "What did they do to you?" Then it paled slightly and seemed to sag. "I trust you. If he wants to, he can live with us."

"Will," Goodnight said, his voice subdued, "I think Two Feathers is with Naldo and the remuda. Go talk to him. Maybe we can get this settled tonight."

Will found Two Feathers working the tangles from Gray Wolf's mane and tail. The grullo no longer shied away when Will got close. He reached under the coarse mane and scratched the muscular neck. "I talked to Pa again."

Two Feathers worked a strand of mane from a particularly tight cocklebur.

"Pa said it would be fine for you to live with us."

"Why?"

"Why what?"

"Why does he want me to live with you?"

While working out a tangle, a grass burr stuck to Will's finger. With a grimace, he pulled it out and flicked it to the ground. "I told him you have no family. I told him I want you to live with us. I told him you are not safe with Yellow Hawk."

"What did he say?"

A grin inched its way across Will's face. "He said he trusted me." Pride swelled up inside him. He looked at Two Feathers, and the grin spread wide.

Two Feathers's nimble fingers stopped picking at the tangles. He gripped the mane. One arm slid over the withers, and he hung onto the grullo. Neither boy spoke.

Will held his breath.

Two Feathers grinned back and nodded.

"We have to start calling you John." Will relaxed. "I don't want the soldiers thinking you belong on the reservation. Hey, where did you go the other day when we went to the fort? I looked for you everywhere."

Two Feathers stroked the sleek mane, now free of tangles, and grinned at Will. "I did not want to go with the soldiers, so I took a ride. A long ride."

By midmorning next day, Pa, Will, and John headed for Fort Sumner. Two Feathers tucked his long braids under Will's old hat and wore a shirt of Tony's and some pants of Jake's. They rode up to the sutler's store and tied the three horses to the hitching rail.

Will's boots echoed in the cavernous room as he walked across the board floor. A mixture of smells greeted him, and he inhaled deeply. Hams hung from the rafters, along with bunches of onions and peppers. Sacks of flour and bags of sugar lined the walls next to barrels of dried beans. Shelves filled with canned goods and tins of herbs and spices lined the wall behind the huge counter. Tables piled high with clothing filled one end of the store.

"Will, you and Two . . . uh, John, come look through these pants. Your clothes won't last much longer."

Pa took his list of supplies to the clerk at the counter, who looked over the top of his glasses at Two Feathers.

"That Indian boy with you?" His voice held a tense edge.

"Yes, he is."

One look at Pa's hard face and the clerk started filling the order.

Will grabbed two pairs of pants and two shirts. He piled them on the corner of the table.

John's hands hung at his sides.

"Hurry up. I want to look around," said Will.

John stared at Will, then blinked several times.

One corner of Will's lips twisted in aggravation. Then realization hit. *He's never been in a store and bought clothes. He's as lost here as I was in the desert.*

Will grabbed a pile of pants and held up several pairs until he found two about John's size. Then he searched through the shirts until John nodded that he liked one, and then another.

They took their clothes to the counter and added them to Pa's growing pile of supplies. Will didn't like the way the clerk sneered at Two Feathers.

"Pa," Will said, "I know I ruined my new hat, but can I get another one? There's not much left of this old one. And John needs one."

"If you promise not to use it for a rattler's hidey-hole."

Will smiled and felt his face flush at the memory of the snake. "Come on, John." They walked to a row of shelves with hats of all sizes and shapes. Will found one just like what Pa had given him.

John looked them over slowly. "Do I have to wear one?" he asked, his voice barely above a whisper.

A couple of soldiers came in the door. Their eyes on John and Will, they went to the counter for a bag of jerky.

Glancing at the clerk, Will whispered, "Yes, you have to look like a cowboy."

They found one darker and slightly larger than Will's. John pulled Will's hat off and his long braids tumbled down his back. He stuffed them under the new hat and set it on the very top of his head, then turned to Will.

Rubbing his cheeks to hide his grin, Will nodded. "We'll work on it when we get back to camp."

"You boys find what you need?" Pa walked up, his arms full of supplies. "Let's get this stuff paid for and get out of here."

Will spotted a row of big jars filled with rock and stick candy in every color and flavor he could imagine lined up on one end of the long counter. "Pa, can we have some candy?"

Pa counted the supplies, and the clerk added up the bill. "Sure. Each of you get five cents' worth."

Will and Two Feathers stared at the jars of brightly colored delight. Will's mouth watered. How could he make a decision with so many choices? Cherry? Peppermint? Horehound? He couldn't make up his mind, so he decided on a little of each.

Two Feathers stared blankly at the jars.

"Hurry up. Pa's about finished adding up the bill."

Two Feathers handed Will his empty sack and shrugged.

"You've never had candy, have you?" Will filled the bag with a variety of colored rocks and sticks. "You're in for a treat."

Carrying the supplies, they headed out. A burly soldier blocked the door.

"Who's this Indian? Is he Apache? He don't look Navajo."

"No, he isn't," Pa said and pushed past the burly soldier, who followed him and the boys out.

The man stood on the porch and watched. Pa fill the saddlebags on all three horses with supplies and hung the rest in bags from the saddle horns.

"Mount up, boys."

"Wait a minute, here," the soldier said and stomped down the porch steps. Grabbing John by the arm, he dragged him away from the grullo. John's sack of candy hit the ground. "This Apache, or whatever he is, ain't leaving this reservation."

With barely controlled fury, Pa gripped the man's shirtfront in one work-hardened hand and a pistol appeared in the other—shoved under the man's chin. "That's *my* boy. Keep your hands off him."

"Mr. Whitaker, what's going on here?" Sergeant Baker from General Carleton's office walked up.

"This soldier manhandled my boys." He gave him what appeared to be a light shove. The soldier hit the ground with a solid thud. With a foot on his chest and a pistol pointed at his throat, the man stayed put.

"So, this is John Randall?" The sergeant put his hand out to shake.

Two Feathers didn't move.

Will stepped up and shook the officer's hand. "I'm Will Whitaker, sir," he said between gulps of air and glances at the man under Pa's foot.

The large, broad-shouldered sergeant looked down at the soldier. "Private Donley, the boy does not belong on this reservation. He is neither Apache nor Navajo."

With laughter dancing in his eyes, he put his hand on Pa's shoulder. "Mr. Whitaker, I'd appreciated it if you'd let this fine soldier up. He has duties elsewhere."

Pa stepped back and holstered his pistol.

The man scrambled up and, with a sneer at John, walked away.

"I'm sorry for any misunderstanding, Mr. Whitaker. You and the boys are welcome. Are you moving on with Mr. Goodnight in the spring?"

"No, we're settling here. We'll be scouting the area for a place to build a ranch."

"This is beautiful country and good for cattle. This land needs strong, stable people. Good luck to you."

Will climbed on the hitching post and jumped onto Buck's saddle. "Come on, John. Let's get out of here and back to camp. I'm hungry."

John walked to Gray Wolf and untied the reins. He stood looking around at the Indians that had gathered when the trouble started. They stood in groups on the porch and around the store.

Pa and John mounted and followed Will toward camp. Buck soon outdistanced the other horses. Will hollered back at the pokey pair. "Hurry up. Those cowboys are gonna eat all Cookie's grub."

After lunch, Will missed Two Feathers and went searching for him. He found him sitting on a low bluff overlooking the Pecos, his arms wrapped around his knees.

"What are you doing out here?"

No answer.

Will sat beside him and studied the stoic face. "What's wrong?"

"How can I live like a white man? I am Comanche. But I do not want to be like the people at the fort."

A dragonfly fluttered by in jerky circles as it headed for the water of the Pecos. Will watched it go by.

"You lived in a cabin with your folks when you were little. Your pa was white. You can do it again." Will dug into his pocket and pulled out the green ribbon, the lock of Old Pony's mane still tied to one end. "When Ma died, my whole world changed. Just like yours did when your folks died. We both did okay. This is her ribbon." He grinned at Two Feathers. Stretching it over his knee, he rubbed out the wrinkles. "I kept this to remember her. I didn't ever want to forget."

He dug again in his pocket and pulled out his pocketknife. Wrapping the ribbon over the blade, he cut off the part with the lock of mane. "Old Pony was all you had to remember your folks. The day he died, I cut this lock of mane and tied it with Ma's ribbon. I know the Comanche don't speak of the dead, but you need something to help you remember your Pa and Ma. So, here. This is yours." He put the lock of mane tied with the green ribbon in Two Feathers's hand.

The sun-browned fist closed over it. Two Feathers rubbed the coarse hair between his thumb and fingers. The boys sat together and watched a dragonfly dip to the water and dart away. The cicadas sang their pulsing song in the afternoon heat.

Two Feathers untied a small, beautifully tanned deerskin pouch from the leather band around his waist and slipped in the keepsake.

"That's a nice bag. Can I see it?" Will held out his hand.

Two Feathers handed it to him.

"I've only held one other thing that felt as soft and fine as this." He grinned. "Buck's muzzle, the day he was born."

"Weeping Woman made it for me." He retied the pouch to the leather band and stood. "Call me John only when we are with whites. My name is Two Feathers." He looked around at the treeless swells and dips of the high desert and the twists and turns of the Pecos. "We are both a long way from home." They stood together, side by side in companionable silence.

"Let's go see about shaping your new hat."

Will headed to camp, and Two Feathers followed.

At daybreak the next morning, Pa, Will, and Two Feathers left their cattle under the watchful eye of a couple of troopers. After saying their good-byes to Mr. Goodnight, Cookie, and the drovers, they headed up the Pecos toward Puerto de Luna. They rode all day, stopping at noon by a little creek that flowed into the Pecos, where they ate the biscuits and beef Cookie had packed for them. Will grinned as Two Feathers wiggled and squirmed, trying to get used to the new clothes and the big saddle instead of his small, simple Comanche rig. That night, they camped under some cottonwood trees in a sharp bend of the river.

About midmorning the next day, the land along the river changed from flat with rolling hills to rugged sandstone bluffs that overlooked the Pecos. The river widened here and flowed deeper than they had seen so far. The land near the river flattened out with sacaton and grama grass that would support cattle. Stands of pine and juniper trees, both up on the flats and down to the Pecos River brakes, would provide winter protection from the wind and snow.

They rode up on the bluffs and looked around. To the east, as far as Will could see, were rolling hills with good grass cover and some mesquite. He thought of their ranch back home. This land was bigger. He thought of the lands he had seen on the trip. This land was richer. He followed Pa away from the river and down a clear running creek to the east. Pa showed him blue grama, side-oats grama, and buffalo grass that grew in abundance.

"What do you think?" Pa pulled up his horse, shaded his eyes from the morning sun, and swept the area. "Good grass and good water."

Will stood in the stirrups, and his eyes seemed to stretch at the vast distance.

Two Feathers rode away from them to the west, crossed the river, and disappeared into one of several groves of old cottonwood trees along the edge of the creek.

Will and Pa sat and talked about the land that lay before them. They pointed out the good points, like good grass and water, and discussed ways they could live with the bad points, like the cold winters and distance from other people and towns.

"This looks good to me," Pa said with a grin. "How about you?"

Before Will answered, Two Feathers hollered and waved for them to come.

They rode along the edge of the creek. It ran shallow but held scattered pools of deeper water. Beautiful layered orange, yellow, and brown sandstone formations lined the banks. On the trails coming down to the water, Two Feathers pointed out tracks of several deer and antelope, as well as small game and birds.

Will looked at Pa. "I like it."

They both looked at Two Feathers.

He smiled. "It is good for a half-white Comanche."

"What are we going to call this new ranch of ours?" Pa's eyebrow raised at the question.

Will looked at the river, winding its way through the trees. He scanned the flat land across the river and the sandstone bluffs on their side. "How about Pecos River Ranch? This river will help us maybe someday move our river of cattle to a market to sell. And besides, Ma would love this place." He took the green ribbon from his pocket and handed it to Pa. "Remember how she wouldn't wear it, except when she dressed up for something special? She always said green was her favorite color."

Pa took the tattered ribbon in his rough, work-worn hands and smoothed out the wrinkles. "Where did you get this? I thought it was lost." His voice was hoarse, and he had to clear his throat to speak.

"I put it in my pocket the day we packed her things. I want to bury it here and plant sunflowers over the spot. That way, it will be like she is here with us."

Pa gave the ribbon back to Will. "That will be fine," he said, his voice husky. "When we build our cabin, we'll pick the perfect spot."

Will looked at Two Feathers. He watched his friend finger the soft deerskin pouch and then shake his head.

Will thought of how many times on the long trip he had reached for the ribbon. *He is not ready to bury Old Pony. It takes time.*

"That settles it," said Pa. "We'll set up camp here. I want to look the land over and go back for the cattle in a few days. Will, get the supplies off the horses. Two Feathers, show us what a good hunter you are and get us some supper."

Two Feathers gave Will the supplies from Gray Wolf, and with his bow and quiver, he crossed the Pecos and followed the creek east.

Will found enough firewood to last the night and for breakfast the next morning. Pa made coffee and was pouring a cup when they heard a shout. They looked up to see Two Feathers splashing across the river. He pulled Gray Wolf to a stop and motioned for them to come.

Two Feathers led them to a spot where the creek banks flattened out. Animal tracks were plentiful in the soft, damp sand.

"What's the matter?" Will asked when they stopped. Two Feathers walked to the edge of the water.

"Look," he said, pointing to the ground.

Pa dismounted and walked over. "Unshod horse tracks." He squatted for a closer look. "Indians watered here several days ago. Most of the Apaches are on the reservation at Bosque Redondo. It must be Comanche."

"Yes," said Two Feathers. "Yellow Hawk."

Will looked at Two Feathers. Every inch of him locked up. Burning fire erupted in the back of his throat. He swallowed. Coughed. Swallowed again. His stomach clinched when that tobacco feeling slammed with a sharp punch.

"How do you know it's Yellow Hawk?" Saying that name swept fear, like shards of glass, through his body. "It could be anyone."

"I trailed him across the desert to find you. I know his horse's track. It is Yellow Hawk."

"Buck," Will said, his voice hard as flint. He dismounted, stiffened his weak knees, and walked over to look at the tracks. "That Comanche wants Buck."

"And he wants me." Two Feathers stepped in front of Will and put his hand on his friend's shoulder. "And now he wants you."

HOME

Morning found Will and Two Feathers huddled over the fire, sipping cups of black coffee. Two Feathers no longer made a sour face when he drank the strong brew. The air held a nip, and the boys lingered over the fire after they'd finished breakfast and helped Pa clean up.

"Saddle up, boys. We have a busy day ahead, so we might as well get started." Will took Two Feathers's cup and rinsed it along with his own, then handed them to Pa to store away in the packs. Pa hung the packs holding their food supplies from a high branch, out of reach of any hungry animals, and stacked the others against a tree trunk.

The sun stretched its bright-orange fingers over the horizon and promised to warm the day. They searched for a spot to make a brush corral to hold their cattle once they brought them from Fort Sumner. With Yellow Hawk in the area, Pa decided they would all stay together, which slowed their search, but Will didn't care. *Does Two Feathers worry about his uncle as much as I do?* he wondered. *I can't ever tell what he's thinkin'.*

They covered the west side of the Pecos toward Puerto de Luna and moved into the area of the sandstone mesas. As they rode, Will thought about Yellow Hawk. *Where is he?* He half expected him to come racing out of an arroyo. He looked at the other two riding beside him. *Pa has his Henry repeater. Two Feathers has his bow and arrows. And I have . . . a pocketknife. Dang it! If I'm going to protect myself, Pa has got to get me a rifle. I'm gonna tell him tonight.*

After about two hours of riding up and down the river and checking every nook and cranny, Pa spotted a draw that led to a wide opening in a break in the rocky mesa. Following the draw through the opening, they discovered a large valley of a couple hundred acres that slanted downhill toward a small lake about three-quarters of the way through the field.

Will and Pa turned to each other, both grinning.

"Think it will do, Pa? There's plenty of grass here."

"Let's take a look." They walked the horses through the waving grass. Pa slowly nodded. "The bluffs nearly surround the field and will block the wind this winter."

Will gave Buck a tap and loped off toward the broken walls that surrounded the field. Pa rode after him.

Will pulled Buck up at the edge of the lake and turned to his father. "Where's Two Feathers?"

"He's checking for trails into this little valley. I told him to be on the lookout for unshod horse tracks."

"Yellow Hawk!" Will sat up straight in the saddle and pulled Buck up short. Sucking in a long breath, he looked at his father and words gushed from his mouth. "Pa, what if Yellow Hawk comes back? I need a rifle. I know Ma didn't want me to have one till I was twelve. But, as you said one time, 'that was then, and this is now.' I didn't need one on the ranch in Texas, but this is New Mexico Territory. I *need* one now."

Mouth hanging open in surprise, Pa sat for a few minutes without speaking, then pulled his hat off and ran his hands through his hair.

"Ya know what, Will? I think you're right. When we get the cattle, we'll see what that old clerk has at the sutler's store."

For the next two days, Will, Pa, and Two Feathers worked cutting and hauling branches, bushes, and anything else they could find to fill breaks in the walls of their natural corral. They cut small trees and lashed the saplings together to make two large gates, one for each end of the valley, that could be moved quickly into place after the cattle passed through.

Everywhere they went, they studied the ground for tracks. Two Feathers drew a picture in the dirt of Yellow Hawk's horse's hoofprint so Will and Pa would know it.

The hard work and long hours took their toll. Will's back and arms ached. His hands stung and itched from scratches. New blisters formed, and old calluses didn't seem so tough. The second night, Pa set pots of water on the fire, and both boys soaked their sore hands in the soothing heat and counted blisters to see who had the most.

Pa reached for the coffee pot and poured a fresh cup. As he put the pot back on the fire, Two Feathers took Pa's hand and turned it over in his. He rubbed the hard calluses and tough skin.

"Cowboy work is hard."

He let go of Pa's hand and put his back in the warm water. A heavy sigh whooshed from his chest.

Will hid his smile.

Sunrise of the third day found them on the trail back to Fort Sumner for their cattle. Will spent the long hours on the trip dreaming. *I wonder what rifles that old clerk has.*

Maybe a Henry, like Pa's. Or a Winchester. Smokey's Sharps .50 is too big. He held his arms up, aimed his imaginary rifle, and "shot" at various targets. As the hours and miles passed, Will's shooting skills improved until he dreamed of bringing home all the meat they could eat and even more for making mountains of jerky.

They rode into the fort the next day and pulled up in front of the sutler's store. Sergeant Baker from General Carleton's office walked through the doorway onto the porch.

"Mr. Whitaker, did you and your boys find a place to your liking?"

Pa shook the soldier's hand. "Yes, we did. We found a good place about halfway between here and Puerto de Luna. We've come to get supplies and move the cattle north."

"Near Puerto de Luna?" He folded a stiff new bandana and slipped it into his back pocket. "That's pretty wild country, but not too far away. Maybe we'll see more of you." The sergeant stepped down from the porch, then turned back to Pa. "By the way, General Carleton wants to see you. He has some news you need to hear." He walked toward the general's office.

"Well, boys, should we see what Carleton wants now or get our supplies first?"

Will looked at the store's wide open door, frowned, and sighed. "I guess we'd better see what news he has. Business comes first."

Two Feathers just shrugged.

General Carleton welcomed them into his office, and they shook hands. This time, Two Feathers shook the offered hand with a smile.

"I have some news I think you folks will like hearing. I received a communiqué from Fort Bascom that Yellow Hawk's band has been captured and is in transit to the Nations. They will be held there until the army decides what to do with them."

Two Feathers grabbed Will's arm in a tight grasp and whispered, "Ask if Yellow Hawk's people were taken."

Will asked the question.

Carleton looked at Two Feathers but spoke to Dan. "A troop of soldiers came up on some women skinning a couple of buffalos. They hid until the women headed to their camp and then followed. They took everyone in the village. There is one problem, however. The report said four or five warriors managed to slip away in the night, but it didn't say who they were."

Will and Two Feathers turned to each other. They both looked at Pa.

"Well, boys. I can't imagine the army letting Yellow Hawk get away."

Will threw his head back, shut his eyes, puffed out his cheeks, and blew out a burst of air. "It sure makes me feel better," he said. "But can I still get my rifle?"

Pa grinned and stood to go. "Thank you, General, for the news. It'll make setting up our ranch a lot easier."

Two Feathers hung his head. He followed Will and Pa to the store and stood in the shadows of a corner until Pa had bought the supplies for the winter and a wagon and team to haul them. Will and Pa looked over the rifles the clerk had on hand and decided on a Henry Carbine. They added several boxes of shells and a rifle boot to their supplies. Will turned to show Two Feathers his gun but couldn't find him. He and Pa looked through the store, then outside.

"There he is," Pa said. Two Feathers stood, leaning against Gray Wolf. "It looks like something is worrying him. You go talk to him while I load the wagon."

"Pa, do you think he's upset because we didn't get him a rifle? Or maybe he's worried about Yellow Hawk?"

"I don't know. Go find out."

Will walked over to the horses. He buckled his rifle boot to his saddle and slipped his new gun inside.

"John, what's wrong? Are you upset because you didn't get a rifle?"

Two Feathers looked at Will, surprise on his face. "No." He stared through the fort gates. "Weeping Woman and . . . " He stopped, ducked his head, and then continued in a voice so low Will could barely make it out. "Red Wing."

Pa drove up with a wagon loaded with their supplies. "Come on, boys, we have a long trip back. Will, you drive the wagon, and John and I will start the cattle. Two vaqueros traveling to Puerto de Luna will meet us up the trail a ways."

Will tied Buck to the back of the wagon and tried to reassure John. "We'll figure something out. Maybe we'll learn more news next time we come to the fort."

Three days later, the cattle poured through the gate into the valley at the Pecos River Ranch. Will and Two Feathers swung the heavy gate and lashed it in place. All three watched the cattle spread out on the grass. The two bulls walked to the water in the middle of the field with their heads swinging, every plodding step accompanied by low moaning bellows of satisfaction.

The next day, Pa called to Will and Two Feathers. "You boys head upriver. See if you can find a good place for a dugout. Winter is heading our way, and we need a warm, dry spot to hole up till spring. Lupe and I will search downriver. Mateo's gonna take the wagon on toward Puerto de Luna to his family's ranch to get logs to frame the front of the dugout." Pa added sternly, "Stay on the lookout, and keep together."

Pa saddled his horse, then helped Will with Buck's rig and gave him a boost up. Two Feathers easily swung himself onto Gray Wolf bareback.

"Remember, boys." Pa stepped into the stirrup and swung his leg over the saddle. "You have to find a place not too high up in the hills, with flat ground around it. Be sure it's big enough to be a barn when we build a regular house next year. Lupe and Mateo said their family will build us an adobe house that will be cool in the summer and warm in the winter."

The boys headed upriver, following the snake-like twists and turns of the Pecos. They came to a game trail that led from the river and up a long rise. It topped out on a flat mesa with views in both directions. They were not far from camp. Will pointed to the river that had fooled them into thinking they had traveled a long way.

The back of the mesa sloped down onto flat land that would make good pasture. A creek wound around a rocky hill, through a grove of cottonwood trees, along the edge of the mesa, and emptied into the Pecos. Where the creek turned away from the hill, they found an area of tumbled sandstone rocks fronting a cave opening. Will scrambled up the rocks to the top of the hill. The game trail led down the slope onto the flat land. In the distance, sandstone bluffs that he figured were the outside walls of their brush corral shone red, tan, and brown in the sunlight.

A muffled call from Two Feathers brought him scrambling back down the rocks. He found him in a cavern at least as large as their cabin back home. Excited, the boys circled the cavern and found it solid, with dry rock walls and floor.

"Two Feathers," Will said as he ran outside, "we could clear away these tumbled rocks and build a good front to the cave." Excited, Will ran in and out of the cavern and from one side of the opening to the other. "Pa can build us a fireplace. The opening is wide enough to put it on one side and run the chimney up the outside. I think it would work, don't you? The one he built in Texas never smoked or anything. He's a pretty fair cook, too."

Two Feathers looked at the rocks lying in a heap, then at the cave opening. After studying the opening and climbing up and down the pile of rocks, he scrambled to the hill over the cave and studied the sky and the surrounding area. "The wind blows from the north in the winter and from the south in the summer. The wind will not come down the chimney and smoke the fire. It is a good place."

The boys followed the game trail away from the Pecos as it meandered across the flat desert. They got back to camp in about half the time it had taken them when they followed the twisting river.

Pa was back, and a pot of coffee simmered on the edge of the fire. Lupe patted round tortillas in his hands and cooked them in the bottom of a skillet, while a pot of beans seasoned with strips of jerky simmered in a Dutch oven.

"We found it! The perfect spot." Will's voice squeaked with excitement. "Boy, are you going to be surprised. It's a rock cave with a creek nearby. It's perfect. Come on. We'll show you." In his eagerness, Will dashed back and forth between the horses and the fire.

Pa laughed.

Two Feathers rolled his eyes as he watched Will.

"Let's wait till lunch is over," said Pa. "Then we'll go take a look."

Later that afternoon, they rode to the back of the mesa, followed the creek around the hill, and Will showed him the cave with the tumbled sandstone rocks. Pa walked all around, inside and out. Will watched as he studied the lay of the land and figured the slope and drainage. He paced off the opening and planned the placement of the timbers to support the roof of the porch and how many timbers it would take to close in the opening of the cave. They picked the best spot for the stone fireplace.

"What about the horses, Pa? Buck needs a warm home." Will burst into a fit of laughter. "I guess he'll have to stay in the cabin with us."

Pa laughed, too. "I may ride a horse all day, but I'm not sleeping with him all night." He decided a second door just past the fireplace, and a short wall from the back of the chimney to a corner of the cave, would make shelter for Buck, Gray Wolf, and his bay. The other horses he bought from Charlie Goodnight would stay in the rope corral with the cattle.

"I saved the best for last." Will beckoned for Pa to follow.

They all walked to the grove of cottonwood trees that flanked the creek. Even after the dry summer, there was plenty of water. At the edge of the trees, an open area spread out like a fan from the direction of the cave to the edge of the creek. At the base of the fan, the remains of a small rock house lay in scattered heaps. Only a portion of two walls remained standing, but the sandstone slabs used to construct it lay scattered throughout the trees. The place was shady and cool. Birds twittered in the treetops, and the front of the cave could easily be seen from where they stood. Not far from one of the remaining walls, isolated from the others in the grove, stood a particularly large cottonwood tree. The grass around the base was lush.

"What do you think, Pa? Would this be a good place for a cabin? It's not far from the brush corral. It's close to the cave, and there's plenty of water."

Pa studied the area for a long time. He walked from the old cabin to the creek and back. He walked from the cabin to the cave and back. He stood behind the grove of trees and looked toward the brush corral. Then he grinned at Will.

"I believe we are home."

The next afternoon, Mateo returned with the timbers and two of his older boys to help with the work. Two weeks later, the front of the dugout was rainproof and windtight. Will and Two Feathers's fingers hurt from the work of tightly lashing the bed frames, chairs, and a table together, all under the watchful eyes of Lupe and Mateo. The rough furnishings provided all the comforts of home, even if they lacked in beauty.

As Mateo, Lupe, and his sons rode toward Puerto de Luna and home, Will called out, "Nos vemos en la primavera."

Pa looked at Will in surprise. "What did you say?"

"See you in the spring," Will said, walking off with a swagger. "Mateo taught me."

The boys and Pa packed up their camp and settled the horses in their new home.

"Pa," Will said as he picked up his blankets. "I'm glad we get to sleep inside tonight. It was so cold last night, and I hugged that fire so close I thought my blankets would burn up."

For the next week, Will worked on a secret project. Every chance he got, he slipped off to the large cottonwood tree. Settled against the trunk, and using his pocketknife on a block of juniper, he worked on a small wooden box. He carved *Joanna Whitaker* on the lid.

When he finished the box, he took the tattered green ribbon from his pocket and washed it in the clear water of the creek. Spreading it on the hearth to dry, he set the box in the middle of the table and waited for Pa to notice it.

"What's this?" Pa said as he sat down with his cup of coffee.

"I made it." Will picked it up and handed it to his father.

Two Feathers came and sat down. "What is it?"

"It's a box for Ma's ribbon. If I keep carrying it in my pocket, there won't be anything left of it."

"It's beautiful." Pa rubbed his work-roughened hands over the letters. Turning it over and over, he slid his fingers across the smooth wood. "You did a good job."

"I'm going to bury it and plant sunflowers over it."

"No." Two Feathers walked to his pack and took out the small, soft leather pouch. Taking the ribbon from the hearth, he brought them both to the table. "Do not put it in the ground."

Will looked at Pa, then at Two Feathers. Irritation twitched the corners of his mouth. No one could tell him what to do with his mother's ribbon.

Two Feathers held the pouch and looked at Will. "When you gave me this gift, you said I needed something to remember my father and my mother. You said my father had given me . . . " he stopped and took a deep breath, "my horse, and as long as I had him, I would have my father and mother."

Will's anger slipped away as he listened.

"It is the same with you." Two Feathers picked up the ribbon. "This belonged to your mother. As long as you have it, you will have your mother." He folded the ribbon carefully and put it in Will's box. Then he opened the pouch and took out the strands of mane Will had cut from Old Pony.

Will gasped. Two Feathers had taken the long hairs, braided them into a tight string, and tied each end with thin, fine strips of leather. From the leather ties on one end hung two small, white dove feathers. Will held it gently in his hands. The fine workmanship showed the same level of care Two Feathers had given to his faithful friend.

Two Feathers handed the box to Will and went to the mantel Pa had set into the stone of the fireplace. He laid his pouch in the center.

Will took his box and put it beside the pouch. He looked at Pa. "I have sunflower seeds. I brought them from home. Ma and I were going to plant them beside the steps."

"Why don't we plant them along the front porch of the adobe house we'll build in the spring? I think she would like that."

Will smiled and nodded.

Pa, Will, and Two Feathers raced the changing seasons to have enough fuel, food, and fodder for the cold winter ahead. They cut wood. Two Feathers quickly learned to swing the axe and send the split wood flying.

They hunted. Will hunted rabbit and an occasional deer. His marksmanship improved with time, but Two Feathers still brought home more meat.

They gathered. Will found walnut trees. He collected all the nuts he could shake down from the trees. Two Feathers showed them how to collect and harvest the pinyon seeds.

They stacked. Any tall grass they came across fell victim to the scythe as they cut, dried, and piled it in haystacks.

The days got shorter, and the nights got colder. The sound of the crackling fire and its warmth, the smell of baking bread, and the laughter that bounced off the walls of the cave filled Will with the comfortable feeling of home.

A feeling he'd missed during the long months trailing behind the river of cattle.

~THE END~

ABOUT THE AUTHOR

 Alice V. Brock learned to love Western books as a child when her father brought home a Louis L'Amour paperback Western and she fell in love with the cowboys galloping through those pages. Mr. L'Amour's books, and TV shows like *Gunsmoke*, *Rawhide*, and *Bonanza* of the late '50s and '60s, brought the West alive to her. The history of Texas and the Old West is full of real stories of those times. Her wish is to bring them alive for kids of today. The Old West has not disappeared, and Alice brings real people in the history of Texas and the Old West to her writing. Real people who lived in history and have descendants who live today.

Her chance to see cowboys in action came when she married and moved to her husband's family ranch in Iola, Texas, where she watches the grazing cattle from her kitchen window. Her grandchildren are the fifth generation to live on the Brock Ranch.

To learn more about Alice V. Brock and her writing, visit her website at www.AliceVBrock.com. Watch for announcements about the next book in the Will and Buck series, *Murder on the Pecos*.

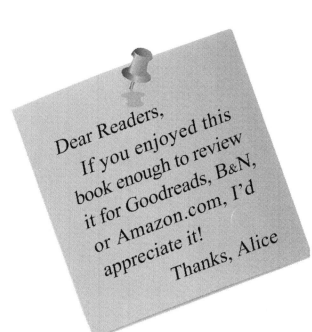

Dear Readers,
If you enjoyed this book enough to review it for Goodreads, B&N, or Amazon.com, I'd appreciate it!
Thanks, Alice

Find more great reads at
Pen-L.com

Made in the USA
Columbia, SC
01 June 2018